MW01256116

The Mysterious Case of the Missing Crime Writer

RAGNAR JÓNASSON

Translated from the Icelandic
by Victoria Cribb

MINOTAUR BOOKS
NEW YORK

First published in the United States by Minotaur Books, an imprint of St. Martin's Publishing Group

EU Representative: Macmillan Publishers Ireland Ltd, 1st Floor, The Liffey Trust Centre, 117-126 Sheriff Street Upper, Dublin 1, DO1 YC43

www.minotaurbooks.com

The Library of Congress Cataloging-in-Publication Data is available upon request.

ISBN 978-1-250-40826-6 (hardcover)
ISBN 978-1-250-40827-3 (ebook)

Our books may be purchased in bulk for specialty retail/wholesale, literacy, corporate/ premium, educational, and subscription box use. Please contact MacmillanSpecialMarkets @macmillan.com.

This book has been translated with financial support from:

 ICELANDIC LITERATURE CENTER

Originally published in Iceland with the title *Hvítalogn* by Veröld Publishing: 2023

First English-language edition published in Great Britain by Penguin Michael Joseph, a part of the Penguin Random House group of companies: 2025

First U.S. Edition: 2025

10   9   8   7   6   5   4   3   2   1

Katrín Guðjónsdóttir
(1950–2023)
In memory of my beloved mother

Special thanks are due to Jónas Ragnarsson
and Hulda María Stefánsdóttir for reading
over the manuscript, and to Dr John Curran for
his suggestions of golden-age crime novels for
Helgi Reykdal's reading list.

Also by Ragnar Jónasson

Snowblind

Nightblind

Blackout

Rupture

The Darkness

The Island

The Mist

The Girl Who Died

Outside

Reykjavík (with Katrín Jakobsdóttir)

Death at the Sanatorium

Helgi Reykdal's Reading List

Agatha Christie (1890–1976): *Peril at End House* (1932)
S. S. Van Dine (1888–1939): *The Dragon Murder Case*
    (1933)
Anthony Berkeley (1893–1971): *Cicely Disappears*
    (The Wintringham Mystery)* (1927)
John Dickson Carr (Carter Dickson) (1906–77):
    A Graveyard to Let (1949)
Josephine Tey (1896–1952): *Brat Farrar* (1949)

Morgunbladid newspaper,
15 October 2002

Publication Day for Elín's Tenth – and Final – Book

Today sees the publication of Deadline, *the latest novel by best-selling author Elín S. Jónsdóttir. It is Elín's tenth book and, she has revealed, her last. 'Ten books in twenty years is more than enough,' Elín declared in a brief chat with* Morgunbladid. *'From now on I'm going to devote myself to reading.' The author, who turned sixty earlier this year, published her first book in 1984. The work in question,* White Calm, *was recently included in a list of the best crime novels of the twentieth century by Norway's* Aftenposten *newspaper. Elín has been hailed as a pioneer of Icelandic crime writing. She has received numerous awards for her books, which have sold millions of copies around the world. Three years ago, plans were announced for a TV series based on the novels, a co-production between Germany and the UK. Filming is already well under way on what's anticipated to be the most expensive series ever adapted from an Icelandic work of fiction, and the first episodes, based on* White Calm, *are due to be aired next year. According to Rut Thoroddsen, Elín's Icelandic publisher, the rights to the new novel,* Deadline, *have already been sold to twenty countries.*

2005

[hissing]

I'm happiest in that vague borderland
between daylight and shadows; that's where
I go in search of stories to tell,
particularly stories about crimes. I used
to read all kinds of books before I began
writing myself, and what I noticed was that
the ones that really held my attention, that
made the most indelible impression on me,
were the ones that were concerned with
justice and punishment. That's the theme of
most novels, one way or another; crime is
the driving force of the narrative, even if
we're reading about something quite
unrelated along the way. I suppose I must
have been about thirty when I set about
systematically working my way through the
detective fiction canon, starting with

Agatha Christie, Dorothy L. Sayers and other classic authors of the twenties and thirties, before moving on to the Swedish husband-and-wife team Sjöwall and Wahlöö, whose stories were hugely popular at that time in the seventies, then anything I could find on the bookshelves of friends and relatives.

What sort of thing do you read nowadays?
I read very widely. Whenever I have a free moment, I pick up a book. It keeps me going, keeps me young. That's what books are for: they help you travel to places you wouldn't otherwise be able to visit, journey through worlds that don't exist. At Christmas all I want from my friends are books; there's no other feeling as tantalizing as opening a parcel containing a volume you haven't yet read or weren't even aware existed. For me, Christmas is basically a good book, and it's the same with holidays – they're just an excuse for me to indulge my passion for reading in new surroundings.

Which gives you more pleasure, Elín, writing books or reading them?

[pause]

4

That's an excellent question. I don't
remember being asked that before. Although
I never feel more alive than when I'm
writing, I'd be the first to admit that
reading is easier. Less effort, more
relaxing, which is how it should be, of
course. But I've never regarded writing
as work; it's too enjoyable for that. A
blank page is like a challenge that I feel
compelled to take up. Of course, I started
writing long before my first book was
published, but that was just for my drawer
and will never see the light of day. It's
for my eyes only. And I still write for
myself, for my own entertainment.

**Speaking of which, you stopped after ten
crime novels in . . .**
Ten novels about crimes, yes.

**Ten novels about crimes, in almost twenty
years. One book every two years, as
regular as clockwork.**
As clockwork? I don't know if that's a good
analogy. A clock ticks a lot faster than me.

But then you stopped?
Yes, it was enough. The series was
complete and I was satisfied with the final
shape.

Did it never occur to you to write one more, or even two? Just to take advantage of the momentum, to ride the wave of your popularity?

Never. I won't pretend that I planned it that way from the beginning, from my first book, but after two or three I began to calculate how old I'd be after ten – I'd be twenty years older – and that seemed like a suitable time to stop. Then the series began to take on an overall shape. Really, I should be grateful that I was given the chance to finish it.

I've heard that you write your books longhand or at least that you used to in the early years.

Yes, right up to the last. That's how I was taught to write when I was young, to write stories, physically wielding a pen. I used to do it for my own amusement. I still sit at this desk, in this shabby old chair, and write by hand. You may have noticed that the computer is placed behind me, not on the desk itself. That's the way it should be. You should only use it for assistance. I regard the computer as no more than a reference tool.

You were over forty when your first crime novel came out in 1984, and you'd never had anything published before that, not even a short story in a newspaper or magazine. Its appearance took everyone by surprise. It's unusual to start writing that late, isn't it?

Unusual, maybe, I suppose I'll have to concede that, but I think sometimes you need a degree of maturity before taking a step that large. Because publishing a book is no joke, you know. It isn't so much the writing, it's having to share your thoughts with anyone who cares to read them that's the hard part, even if we're talking about fiction. After all, there's always a grain of truth in every novel. Incidentally, since you brought up the question of age, P. D. James started writing crime novels relatively late, when she was in her forties, and she's still at it, and only gets better with age. Anyway, writing makes me happy. It feels good to create something. For me, the pleasure lies in the physical act of writing, getting the text down on paper – quite literally, as I said. On the other hand, there's nothing more tedious than having to reread your own work. With every edit, something dies inside you – it's like

losing a little piece of yourself each
time. Meanwhile the hourglass is running
out and you can see your soul reflected
there; watch it gradually trickling away.
Only then do you fully understand the
meaning of lost time.

[pause]

Has it been an enjoyable journey?
It's not over yet. I'm still going strong,
though I'm not producing any novels. I
still love all the buzz around it, love
telling people about my books and chatting
to my readers both here in Iceland and
abroad. Though I travel less often than I
used to, I still make the odd trip. It's
a wonderful feeling to have reached so
many readers, perhaps encouraged someone
who didn't read much before to pick up
a book. Introduced them to the magic of
literature.

**Sjöwall and Wahlöö also wrote exactly ten
books. Is that where the idea came from?**
You know, that question isn't quite as
original as the one you asked before.
I've answered it so often. Sjöwall and
Wahlöö didn't have exclusive rights to
that number, but I probably did have the

thought at the back of my mind. Like so many other good authors, they taught me to write about crime, though personally I think I have more in common with Christie and Sayers.

You've lived alone in recent years, haven't you? For most of your life, in fact? Is it a solitary existence or do the books keep you company?

[pause]

If you don't mind, I'd rather not go into that. I've kept my personal life out of the limelight, as you know. Let's just stick to books for now.

[pause]

Looking back, do you have any regrets?
I suggest we take a short break here. We can carry on afterwards.

[hissing]

THURSDAY

2012

Thursday, 1 November

This was Helgi Reykdal's happy place.

The worn but comfy chair in the corner, where he could quite literally breathe in the sweet smell of old books. Hardbacks, paperbacks, they covered the walls and were stacked in piles on the floor and most other surfaces in the shop. There were books everywhere, and if things went on like this, with more coming in than out, it wouldn't be long before the aisles filled up and any visitor would merely be in the way, hardly able to move between the stacks. In fact, you could say the books had long ago gained primacy in the shop, which seemed to have taken on a life of its own, independent of owners, staff or customers. Piles of books for books' sake, not because there was any likelihood of them being sold.

The air was thick with dust, but this didn't bother Helgi, who found the mess charming rather than oppressive. The shop was closed, he was alone in here and the only hint that it was the twenty-first century outside was the mobile phone lying on top of the pile beside him.

At around the time Helgi split up from his long-term girlfriend, Bergthóra, he'd learnt that the woman who had bought the family's second-hand bookshop in the little northern town of Akureyri was struggling to make ends meet and wouldn't be able to honour the final payment.

Things had a way of all happening at once, but instead of being downhearted by these developments, Helgi tried to look on the bright side. His break-up was a good thing, from any point of view. He and Bergthóra had no children and their relationship had run its course a long time ago. The final straw had come when she attacked him with a wine bottle in a drunken rage, smashing it over his head so hard that he had blacked out.

Then there was the shop. His father had spent many hours sitting in this very chair, dipping into books with Helgi at his feet, first as a child, later as an adolescent, being introduced to the magic of stories. He had so many memories from this little shop, which meant more to him than almost anywhere else in the world. Sadly, not many other people appreciated the treasures it contained. They'd had an awful job selling the place after Helgi's father died, and now, as the majority owner, Helgi found himself back in the lap of his memories. The middle-aged woman who had attempted to buy the place still held a small share. She and Helgi had agreed that she could stay on and run the shop on a day-to-day basis, in return for a percentage of the book sales, though these tended to be meagre at best.

Since fate had willed it that the bookshop should end up back in the hands of Helgi's family, he had no intention of selling it again. Some of his colleagues dreamt of retiring to the sun, opening a small bar or B&B perhaps, but he pictured himself here in his later years. Behind the counter like his late father, selling books to invisible customers. The key was to regard it as a vocation rather than a job.

But all that was in the future. For now, Helgi had the shop to himself. He had come across a rare old Icelandic translation of Agatha Christie's *Peril at End House* and had settled down to read it, though he wasn't really concentrating on the plot so much as savouring the atmosphere. Perfect peace, surrounded by books, and only a week left of what had turned into a sort of winter holiday. He had come up north to stay with his mother, who had recently been discharged from hospital. And although he didn't waste any time thinking about Bergthóra these days and had long ago stopped responding to her messages, he couldn't deny that it was good to get away from Reykjavík for a bit. To say that Bergthóra hadn't taken their breakup well would be an understatement; for a while she had refused to accept it. At least here in Akureyri there was less chance of running into her.

He'd been forced to move and make a new start, and had tentatively embarked on a new relationship too. The girl's name was Aníta. They'd met briefly earlier that year, just after he had joined the police. Aníta worked for the Directorate of Health and had helped him with his investigation into the deaths at the old sanatorium outside Akureyri. A couple of weeks later she'd got in touch to ask how the case had gone and they had met up for coffee. By then Helgi had broken it to Bergthóra that they had no future together, though it had taken a while longer to close that chapter of his life.

Now the next chapter had begun. He and Aníta had been together for three months, but he hadn't introduced her to his mother, not yet. They both wanted to take things slowly. Aníta had stayed behind in Reykjavík to work, though they had discussed the possibility of her coming north to Akureyri with him at Christmas.

At that moment Helgi's reverie was shattered by the ringing of his phone. He had forgotten to mute it as he usually did when he was reading. When he was off duty, he found that, as a rule, most things could wait.

His heart sank when he saw that the caller was his boss from Reykjavík CID.

Helgi laid the Agatha Christie down as gently as if it were a fragile treasure and took a deep breath before answering.

'Helgi, Magnús here. How's it going?' The greeting was friendly enough but there was an undertone there that Helgi didn't entirely like.

'I'm fine, thanks. Still up north.'

'Yes, right. And your mother, is she improving?'

'She's getting there.' His mother, who had been undergoing rehabilitation following an operation, was making slow but steady progress.

'I'm very reluctant to bother you during your break, but it occurred to me that you might like . . . how shall I put it? . . . the chance to jump on board a case.'

Helgi rolled his eyes and got to his feet. The atmosphere had been ruined. Whatever it was that Magnús wanted, he suspected it would mean returning to Reykjavík sooner than planned.

'Fire away,' he said, rather curtly, but then it wasn't always easy to hide one's feelings.

'The thing is, knowing that you're such a fan of crime fiction . . .' Magnús said, no doubt by way of introduction to the real business.

'That's right,' Helgi replied, well aware that his colleagues sometimes made fun of his passion. He invariably carried a book around with him and spent any free time at the station reading instead of chatting to people in the coffee room.

He glanced around him. The shelves were sagging under their tempting load and he felt an almost overwhelming urge to hang up on his boss.

'Well, it just so happens that an author has gone missing,' Magnús said.

'What?'

'A crime novelist, what's more. It occurred to me that it would be right up your street.'

At first Helgi thought he must have misheard, then he wondered if Magnús was taking the mickey out of him, for reasons that were obscure.

'Who's gone missing? I'm not with you.'

'Elín S. Jónsdóttir. You'll know the name.'

'Of course I do.' It would be no exaggeration to say that pretty much anyone who read books would know who she was. Her novels, all ten of them, had sold by the truckload over the last thirty years. She had set out to write crime fiction in Icelandic long before the genre had become such an unmissable feature of Iceland's Christmas book flood, and she'd gradually built up a readership until her novels became instant bestsellers on publication, every other year. And she was no less popular abroad. Then she had abruptly stopped writing on the grounds that her series was complete and she 'had nothing more to say', as he remembered her once putting it in an interview. Naturally, he'd read all her books. There were bound to be copies on the shelves surrounding him at this moment. 'Has she literally disappeared?' he asked.

'Without a trace, I think I can safely say. Her publisher got in touch. No one's heard from her for several days and she's not at home.'

Helgi's imagination instantly took flight. He didn't know Elín personally, he'd never met her, but the case fired up his interest to such a degree that he was even prepared to cut short his holiday and return to Reykjavík. It was the link to literature, the intriguing fact – if he were honest – that a crime novelist should become the subject of a criminal investigation.

What's more, he had to admit to himself that he was secretly thrilled at the chance to take part in or even run an investigation that would be in the media spotlight. Missing-persons cases didn't always attract much attention in Iceland; often they were private tragedies that had no public interest angle, and reporters tended to keep their coverage to a minimum, but there was no way this news would go under the radar, whatever lay behind it.

'That's unbelievable,' he said. 'Terrible. Are there any clues to what might have happened?'

'It's all very recent; the notification has only just landed on my desk. Luckily, the press haven't got wind of it yet, and I've still got to assign the case . . .'

The offer dangled in the air.

'I'll take it,' Helgi said decisively. 'I can head back to town today, be with you by this evening.' Excitement bubbled up inside him. This was what it was all about: the chance to tackle demanding cases, under pressure, and emerge victorious.

'I'm delighted to hear it. Why don't you fly? You can fetch your car later. We can't afford to let the trail go cold, Helgi.'

He considered this for a moment and realized that Magnús was right. At least it would give him an excuse to fly back up north at his employer's expense to fetch his car and he'd be able to pay his mother another visit at the same time. He could always borrow a police vehicle while in town.

His mother would understand.

'OK, I'll be with you this afternoon.'

'Now you're talking, Helgi. I doubt anything's going to happen over the next couple of hours but after that the ball's in your court. Mind you, for all we know she may suddenly pop up at lunchtime, back from a holiday or something like that. If not, we'll just have to pull out

all the stops and be ready with some answers, show that
we're taking it seriously. I think we should give ourselves
a few days to solve it before issuing a press release. We'll
be under a lot of pressure from the public. But you can
handle it, Helgi.'

Helgi had a horrible feeling that this was the explanation for the phone call: Magnús wanted a scapegoat to
take the heat if the author didn't turn up soon. Whereas it
went without saying that Magnús would get all the credit
if the mystery was solved quickly and successfully.

'But don't worry, you have my complete confidence,'
Magnús added, in that smarmy tone of his. 'Anyway, it
may just be a false alarm. Maybe . . . er . . . maybe she got
lost in one of her own books.'

2005

[hissing]

As the years pass and one gets older,
one's thoughts tend to become more
preoccupied with time. At least, mine do.
It's unsettling wondering what I could
have changed. Could I have lived my life
differently? You're still relatively
young, so it probably hasn't sunk in
yet . . .

**Yes, it has. We only get one life so we
should live it well.**
Yes, I couldn't have put it better myself.
One life, so . . .

[pause]

Would you like to take a break? Shall I switch off the tape recorder?

No, there's really no need. Sorry for the hesitation. You'll edit it as you think best. Make me look good.

Of course. Anyway, I didn't mean to interrupt. Didn't mean to upset your flow . . .

[pause]

Time, ah yes, that's what I was talking about. Live life well, you said, but sometimes we need to break with habit, smash a few eggs along the way, do something unexpected. Take a chance. You know?

Yes.

Listen to your heart. That's vital. Often you don't even know what your heart is saying. The messages are confused, misleading, the road is winding, the way is never straight, and that's all fine. Right and wrong depend on one's perspective. Sometimes, though not always. In some cases, the line is perfectly clear, but we can talk about that at the end. Oh, can I offer you a refill?

No, I'm fine, thanks. To tell the truth, I'm more of a tea drinker.
Oh dear, you should have said so. I'll put the kettle on in a minute.

Were you listening to your heart, Elín, when you gave up your job as a teacher and devoted yourself to making a living as a writer instead?
I've never thought of writing as 'making a living'. I write for fun; I revel in the process: it's a game, a passion, not a job.

[pause]

I'll tell you something else. When I was a little girl, I lived in the west end of Reykjavík, on the top floor of a block of flats, in a bedroom with a dormer window. It was almost like in a fairy tale: the princess in her tower in a great castle, though really my parents only owned our little attic flat. I used to sit there in the evenings – I suppose I'd have been about ten years old – gazing out over Reykjavík, an entirely different prospect from today, of course: no University Cinema, no National Library, just an unclaimed wonderland for a child with a fertile imagination. That's where this

author, Elín S. Jónsdóttir, had her
origins. I didn't know it then, but I
can see it now, all these years later.
That's how we come into being as people.
We're shaped by our environment, by
our memories, by the infinite number of
decisions we make every day. I decided,
for example, to invite you to take an
interview with me, and who knows where
that will lead?

**Well, it'll . . . the interview will end up
in the papers, of course. I still have to
decide which one, but I'm confident they'll
be fighting over it. A long interview
with the country's favourite author.
It shouldn't be too difficult to find a
suitable publication.**
When the time comes, yes.

Er, right. Um, how do you mean?
Can you picture her?

I'm sorry, who?
The little princess in her attic window.
She's gazing out over the wide expanse
of the city, playing at make-believe,
inventing tales about little princes
and princesses who fall in love, though
they're not always destined to be

together. At first, the tales are of that
sort – romantic, tragic – then gradually
they become a little darker: stories
about moral frailty, the danger inherent
in human beings, stories about crime, in
other words. Can you picture her there?
In the fullness of time, she moves out
of her castle, goes to school, meets her
people. You may not get to choose your
family, but at least you can choose your
friends. Then she goes to university,
intending to read law because her uncle
was a lawyer and everyone looked up to
him; he lived in a beautiful house with
a big garden. She wanted to be like her
uncle. But that wasn't to be. Sometimes
we have dreams that remain forever
unfulfilled – that's life, after all.
The important thing is to have those
dreams. To put them to the test.

[pause]

**Did you go to teaching college at that
point?**
Not straight away. I taught at a school in
the countryside first; took a little break
from the rat race. I don't know what you'd
call it today. Perhaps you would describe
it as a way of grounding myself.

I like that: grounding yourself.
Yes. That was my best year.

Where was this?
Up in the West Fjords. In Ísafjördur. Have
you ever been there?

**No, I don't think so. Not that I can
remember.**
No, that's the thing, one doesn't always
remember. Maybe you went there when you
were very young. Anyway, take it from
me, it has a spectacularly beautiful
setting, like being poised between heaven
and earth. You should visit it sometime,
experience the place for yourself. I
haven't been there for what feels like
forever.

You said you were teaching there?
Yes, at the school. No one would remember
me these days; it was many years ago. I
turned up out of the blue, did my bit,
experienced the town, the mountains, the
sea, got a sense of the local people's
energy, then I just . . . well . . .

[pause]

I disappeared again . . . That's important
too sometimes – the ability to make a

fresh start. To do a disappearing act
and turn up somewhere else. In my case,
I simply went back to Reykjavík, found
myself a new direction in life and
trained to become a teacher. At the time,
I thought that was life. But then, you
know, life is so many things. Not just
one path, one strand, but a series of
coincidences, of feelings. And then, as
it happens, I started to write. Out of
nowhere, really; first in secret, not even
telling my friends. I threw that first
manuscript away, tore it to pieces, flung
it in the bin, then started again. Told
the same story, but from a different point
of view, and it dawned on me that everyone
has their secret, something that can never
be told. Once I'd understood that, I found
it easy to write those ten books.

[pause]

You know, sometimes I think life is just
one big crime novel.

[hissing]

1965

'No, we're not joking. At least, I'm not; I'm deadly serious. I don't just think it's a good idea, I think it's a great idea. Practically risk-free.'

He slammed down his mug for emphasis, as if adding an invisible exclamation mark. The coffee he'd made for his guests was far too strong, but perhaps strong coffee was exactly what was needed to put heart into them.

'You're talking about robbing a bank!'

'You make it sound bad, but I've looked into every angle. Listen, I go to that branch all the time: it's a long way from the nearest police station, they don't have a security guard, and lots of big businesses have accounts there, which means large sums are paid in regularly. We'll find a quiet time, early in the morning, not right at the beginning of the month, and it'll be a piece of cake, guys – a piece of cake.'

'And just how do you two see it happening? Because there's absolutely no way I'm taking part; no chance you're going to fool me into joining you. I'm not spending the rest of my life in jail.'

'I reckon we'll need a gun; I can provide one. My family owns a shotgun. I don't think anyone knows I'm aware of its existence. Afterwards, I'll just quietly put it back. It's kept in an outhouse at our summer cabin – it belongs to my uncle, but he gave up shooting years ago. The whole plan's completely foolproof.'

'OK, I'll take the gun and stand behind you. You do the talking. I bet it'll go like clockwork.'

'Why are you two talking like this? You are pulling my leg, aren't you?'

'It's so much money – it would take us years to earn that much. All it would require is guts and half a morning's work, then we'd be set up for life; no more money worries ever, and . . .'

'For God's sake, money doesn't matter, not in the great scheme of things.'

'We're not doing it just for the money. We're doing it to prove to ourselves that we can. To feel that we're – oh, I don't know – that we're alive. You only live once.'

2012

Thursday, 1 November

Maybe she got lost in one of her own books.

Magnús's bad joke rankled with Helgi.

There were times when he actively disliked his boss, though he tried to conceal the fact. They had little in common and their paths were unlikely to have crossed if fate hadn't willed it that they should work together. Helgi was prepared to bet that Magnús hadn't read a single book by Elín S. Jónsdóttir, though it would be hard to find another Icelander who hadn't. Then again, Magnús probably read nothing but police reports. And for that reason, this investigation, whether it turned out to be a criminal case or not, would be in better hands with Helgi.

He had taken two books with him from the shop, before locking the door behind him.

One was Agatha Christie's *Peril at End House*, mainly to prevent anyone else from buying it, unlikely though that was. He couldn't bear the thought of such a rare treasure ending up in the wrong hands. No one else would appreciate it like he did.

The second title, found after a short search, was a copy of Elín S. Jónsdóttir's debut novel; first edition, first printing. As such, it was a rarity, though first editions didn't go for nearly as much in Iceland as rare books did abroad.

Helgi was intending to dip into the book, maybe read the first few chapters, during the short flight back to Reykjavík, using the time to try and get a sense of the author. It was his belief that all books provided an insight into their author's psyche. After all, it stood to reason that authors must reveal something of themselves in their pages, either deliberately or unconsciously, though no doubt you often had to read between the lines to discover it. Of course, he wasn't expecting this particular book to provide any great revelation about the author's disappearance, but reading it would at least give him a sense of purpose and be better than sitting idle.

He dropped by the house to pack and say goodbye to his mother, explaining that duty called. She didn't seem upset; if anything, she seemed pleased at having a chance to stand on her own two feet after the operation. As a precaution, though, Helgi left her a key to the new flat he was renting in Reykjavík. He felt it was right for his mother to have a key, just in case something happened; once his mother, always his mother. Come to think of it, she probably still had a key to the old flat too, where Bergthóra was now living on her own.

It crossed his mind that he might have gone north

more for himself than for his mother, to savour the smell of the books in the old shop, and – who knows? – perhaps to spend a few days without Aníta to get a bit of distance in which to work out what he felt about this new relationship.

He had been hesitant to make the leap, given how badly things had turned out with Bergthóra, and he had to keep reminding himself that the two women couldn't be more different. That there was nobody else like Bergthóra.

2012

Thursday, 1 November

'Where are you, Helgi? Where the hell are you?'

Aníta was muttering under her breath, biting back the urge to scream. It would be so unprofessional to do so here in her office at the Directorate of Health and risk being overheard by her colleagues.

She had shut the door, but she was still shaking.

She had been trying repeatedly to call Helgi, but his phone seemed to be permanently switched off. Although he was in the north, spending the week with his mother, they usually managed to speak at least once a day. When she'd heard from him that morning he'd sounded in a good mood. She had almost been able to hear him smiling at the other end as he eagerly reported that they'd already had their first snowfall in Akureyri.

She sent him yet another message.

They hadn't known each other long, only a few months, yet she knew it wasn't like him to be uncontactable like

35

this. It wasn't that she was worried about him; she was just in such a state that she was desperate to talk to him. The unexpected visit had left her feeling badly shaken.

Aníta hadn't said anything to her colleagues, just asked her unwanted visitor to leave, then closed the door of her office. She would have to pull herself together so she could complete the rest of her day's work. There was no way she was going to run away home in the middle of the day.

She simply needed to talk to somebody to stop her heart racing like this, and the only person she could discuss it with was Helgi.

But now, for the first time since they'd started seeing each other, she couldn't get hold of him.

A spark had been ignited when he first came to see her while making inquiries for an investigation. Later, she had got in touch with him to ask if he had made any progress in the case. He had been friendly and invited her out for a coffee, which had turned into their first date. Since then, things had progressed and their relationship seemed to be going well. She was counting down the days until he got back to Reykjavík.

When Aníta stood up, her head swam and for a moment she thought she was going to faint. She should probably have stepped outside into the cold, fresh air and gone for a coffee at a nearby café to soothe her nerves, but she couldn't summon up the courage, not yet. She needed a few more minutes to calm down.

She looked out of the window. Even through the glass she could tell how cold it was from the bundled-up figures of the passers-by and the naked branches of the trees. On days like these she couldn't help wishing she lived somewhere else, somewhere warmer. She had raised the subject once or twice with Helgi, asking if he would ever consider moving back to the UK, where he had done his postgraduate studies. He had reacted well to the question, as he did to everything they discussed. There was a warmth and friendliness to their interactions that she really appreciated. And she longed to feel that warmth now, down the phone from Akureyri.

She felt so alone and vulnerable.

She selected his mobile number again, but it was the same story: he didn't pick up.

Where are you?

She was still shaking.

2012

Thursday, 1 November

Helgi managed to make a good start on Elín's book during the half-hour or so that the plane was in the air. He had never particularly enjoyed reading while flying, but he could do it if he had to. At least it was better than reading on car journeys, which made him feel sick. The problem was that he liked to read in congenial surroundings, as that gave rise to the best associations. But travelling by air was the last place you'd look for comfort. The stench of high-octane fuel, the cramped seats, the deafening roar, none of this was a worthy background for a good book.

The novel turned out to be as engaging as he'd remembered, a strong debut from an author who had gone on to be hugely successful. He felt he'd got to know Elín a little as a result. There was an author photo on the back cover. Elín had presumably been in her forties when it was taken. She had a thin face and wavy, shoulder-length hair. The photo was in black and white, as if to enhance the air of mystery, but the author was smiling faintly at the reader, which detracted a little from the darkness. Helgi had seen recent pictures of Elín, and she had aged, of course, but with dignity, and her expression hadn't changed.

He didn't switch on his phone until he had emerged from the terminal and was on his way to the taxi rank. The city looked bleak on that first day of November, the weather raw and blustery. Back in Akureyri, winter had already arrived, but here at Reykjavík's domestic airport on Vatnsmýri it was still autumnal, though the damp cold pierced him to the bone. At times like this he preferred the north.

Next moment, he was stopped in his tracks by the discovery that he had countless unread text messages from Aníta. As he stood there, rooted to the spot, the chill cut through his coat.

Call me.

Where are you?

Please call me.

All the messages were along the same lines. Helgi had never seen this side of Aníta before. Something had to be wrong. He called her.

'Hi, sorry, I was on a plane. I had to fly back early because of work. Is everything all right?'

She didn't immediately answer, then said:

'Your girlfriend, Helgi – your ex-girlfriend, I mean . . .'

He caught his breath.

'Bergthóra? What . . .'

Naturally Aníta was aware of Bergthóra's existence; she'd heard stories about her and the mental abuse she'd subjected Helgi to. He hadn't told her about the physical violence, though, as he couldn't face talking about it.

But Bergthóra didn't know about Aníta.

He hadn't made the relationship public in any way, had only told a few old friends, yet now . . .

'She came to see me at work,' Aníta said. She sounded breathless, as if she was finding it hard to force out the words.

'What? She came to see you at work?' he repeated, unable to believe his ears. An image rose in his mind of the woman who had done her best to ruin his life.

'Yes, Helgi. I was told someone had asked to see me, then she walked into my office. I didn't recognize her at first – she looked different from the photos I've seen. I thought she must be a doctor who wanted to talk to me for some reason, or maybe a patient wanting to lodge a complaint. I was polite to her, but then . . .'

She broke off briefly, before resuming:

'Then she introduced herself. She said her name was Bergthóra and that she was your partner . . .'

'My partner? Is that the word she used?' He felt a cold sense of dread.

'Yes.'

'Are you sure?' he asked, only to regret it immediately. He didn't mean to cast doubt on Aníta's story.

'Quite sure. It totally threw me. And the look on her face as she said it. Like . . .' She hesitated. 'Like she owned you.'

He didn't want to hear any more, but there was no avoiding it.

'Did she say anything else? Or . . .'

41

'Yes. She said she'd heard we were . . . How did she put it? . . . That we'd starting seeing each other, that was it.'

Helgi wondered how the hell she'd got wind of the fact, and – even worse – what she had been intending to achieve by going to see Aníta.

'What did she actually want?' he asked. He was still standing in the biting wind by the terminal building, unable to move until he was satisfied that everything was all right. He added: 'Is everything OK?'

'Yes, I'm just a bit freaked out. To be honest, I didn't know what to think. She gave the impression that you two were still together and that she wanted to remind me of the fact. She told me to stop seeing you, to leave you alone.'

Helgi was stunned. 'She told you to leave me alone?'

'Yes. It was all so strange. There wasn't any doubt, was there? You know, that you . . .'

'There's not a shadow of a doubt that Bergthóra and I are no longer together,' Helgi replied. 'Our relation-ship came to a dramatic end when I walked out on her. I haven't talked to her since or answered any messages from her. Mind you, she's stopped sending them.' The disturbing thought occurred to him that Bergthóra might have stopped hassling him precisely because she was planning to turn her focus on Aníta instead.

'Was she threatening at all?' he asked.

There was a delay, then Aníta said: 'No, not exactly. She didn't threaten me, but it was obvious she wasn't happy that we were seeing each other.'

Helgi thought he could hear a tremor in Aníta's voice.

'I'll have to talk to her.'

'No, please don't. I don't think that's a good idea. She just needs time to get over it, don't you think?'

Helgi heaved a deep breath.

'Yes, maybe.'

'Sorry, I didn't mean to alarm you. I just found the whole thing so unsettling. I'm feeling a bit calmer now, though. Thanks for ringing – I'm definitely feeling better. I'll just tell the receptionists not to let her in again.'

'Yes, you do that. I can't understand what she's trying to achieve.' *Unsettling*, Aníta had said, and he couldn't agree more. 'Do you think she could have been drinking?' he asked. At the time of their break-up, he'd told Bergthóra in no uncertain terms that she should go to rehab, even though it was no longer any of his concern how she lived her life now that their ways had parted. She had reacted badly to the suggestion, insisting that her drinking wasn't a problem. While she was prepared to admit that she sometimes crossed a line when she'd had a drop too much, she claimed that she was perfectly in control when it came to deciding whether or not to open a bottle.

I'm perfectly capable of handling my drink, just like you, she had said, without so much as blinking.

'I'm really not sure,' Aníta said, after a moment's pause. 'It wasn't obvious, but of course people are different and you can't always tell if someone's been drinking.'

Even Helgi hadn't always been able to tell from looking at Bergthóra whether she was drunk; it was her behaviour that gave her away. Her violent outbursts of temper.

'Why don't you go home and take it easy?' he suggested. 'It can't have been a pleasant experience.'

'Oh, no, I'll stay on at work. There's a lot to do, and it wasn't that bad, honestly. I think I can cope with finishing the day.' He heard her laugh but thought it sounded hollow.

'OK, I'll call you later this afternoon or this evening – I don't know how long I'll be.'

They said goodbye.

Helgi was still holding his phone. He started to punch in the first digits of Bergthóra's number, then had second thoughts and shoved the phone back in his pocket. He wanted to ring her and give her a piece of his mind, tell her that behaviour like that was totally out of order. Vent his anger.

But of course that wasn't the right way to handle the situation. It took him a while to realize that this kind of reaction was exactly what Bergthóra was after. She had gone round to see Aníta in order to get his attention, to make him pick up the phone and call her. Well, it wasn't going to work. He had broken off all communication with Bergthóra and he was determined to stick to that decision. Knowing what she was like, he was fairly sure she would only pull that stunt once. Life was like a game of chess sometimes: it was best to plan a few moves ahead. To his regret, he had allowed Bergthóra to dominate the game for far too long; allowed her to go on the attack in the fullest sense of the word, but, thank God, he'd taken control before things could end in disaster.

Common sense would always win out in the end.

There was nothing to be afraid of.

2012

Thursday, 1 November

'Thanks for coming in, Helgi. I need a good pair of hands to take care of this business and I trust you one hundred per cent for the job. I've already taken the first steps on your behalf; I had checks made to see whether she's left the country and apparently she hasn't. I've asked her bank to keep an eye on her accounts too, though her publisher tells me that she mainly uses cash. That's consistent with the small number of transactions on her cards every month. I've also asked for copies of her bank statements, and her account manager is working on that as we speak.'

To outward appearances, Magnús radiated good-humoured matiness, but Helgi wasn't always sure how much faith to put in this facade. He couldn't tell how sincere his boss was. Or, indeed, how good he actually was at his job. People could rise to high positions in spite of limited talents. It was the old story.

'Thanks,' he replied guardedly. He couldn't shake off the feeling that his amiable boss was leading him into a trap, assigning him a case that could prove both challenging and problematic, given that Elín was a well-known public figure.

No doubt he was being unnecessarily cynical, but he reflected that this was hardly surprising given that it was his job to be suspicious of people.

'Yes, I feel confident now,' Magnús continued, 'knowing that the best man in the department is leading the search for Elín.'

This excessive praise bordered on mockery, but Helgi pretended not to notice. He was aware that he had done himself proud during the few months he had been working here since taking over the office of Hulda Hermannsdóttir, a woman he had never met. She had vanished, like Elín, and there was still no news of her fate.

People disappear all the time, Magnús had said that summer, when the search for Hulda was called off. As if the disappearance of a police officer was nothing to make a fuss about. Perhaps his reaction could be explained partly by the fact that the poor woman had been pretty much alone in the world.

'Does she have a family?' Helgi asked, thinking about Hulda.

'I'm sorry?'

'Elín.'

'Oh, Elín. No, I don't think so. From what I can gather, she lives alone. And – get this – she doesn't even use a

46

mobile phone. It seems she's old-fashioned like that. She was supposed to meet a friend on, er, Tuesday, I think it was. Then she failed to turn up to lunch with another friend yesterday. It's Thursday today, isn't it? So no one's heard from her for two days, at least. Her publisher's doing her nut.'

'Shouldn't I go and see her . . . publisher, then?'

'Exactly, yes. That's the plan. Her name's Rut; she's expecting you. She wants to meet you at her home, considering the circumstances.' Magnús slapped Helgi vigorously on the shoulder. 'This is a big case, Helgi, my boy. But it'll be in good hands with you.'

'Yes, sure. People disappear all the time . . . though . . .'

'Hm? Yes, right,' Magnús answered vaguely, and walked unhurriedly away.

1976

Hulda Hermannsdóttir always felt there was a brightness around her little daughter.

She was sitting in the bedroom, on a light April night, watching Dimma sleep. The child was peaceful now, but when she woke up she would be bursting with energy. All Hulda and Jón's time was devoted to keeping an eye on her, but then that was to be expected as parents of a two-year-old.

They shared the chores, as far as possible.

Jón was busy with his investments and Hulda had just gone back to work part-time for the police. They had solved the problem of who would care for Dimma during the day by finding a childminder, an older woman who lived in a basement flat on Miklabraut. She had far more experience in looking after and bringing up children than Hulda and Jón, yet, in spite of this, Hulda never felt happy when she had to leave her daughter with the woman.

Her worries were groundless, of course; it was just that

her bond with her little daughter was so strong. Making sure Dimma was safe was the only thing that mattered.

Hulda would have liked to take a longer maternity leave, but Jón had encouraged her to go back to work, and her old boss was still in his post and keen for her to return as well.

She was all too aware that there was no guarantee her position with the police would still be waiting for her if she stayed away too long.

Her thoughts returned to the sleeping child. Was the name too gloomy, she sometimes wondered. *Dimma*, 'darkness': rather a sinister name for such a beautiful little girl. At the time it had struck Hulda and Jón as an excellent choice, original and memorable. The idea had been his; he'd got it from a book, apparently.

He was already talking about having more children, but, whenever he did, Hulda tried to change the subject. Of course, she adored Dimma, but she wasn't ready for another child, not yet, perhaps never, though she didn't say this to Jón. He was so happy with their daughter. He revelled in being a father, that was undeniable, took an active part in bringing up their child and made an effort not to prioritize work, unlike many men they knew.

Meanwhile, Hulda was ambitious. She was determined to break through the glass ceiling that prevented her from aspiring to the highest ranks in the police.

She was fascinated by the puzzles she encountered at work, stimulated by the drama, the pressure and the darker side of her job.

But she left the darkness behind at work. At home with Dimma, all was sweetness and light.

2012

Thursday, 1 November

'Of course, I don't think there's any particular reason to be alarmed,' Rut, Elín's publisher, said. 'No call to be seriously worried.'

Helgi was at this moment seated in her living room. Like Elín, Rut was around seventy, and looked good for her age. Helgi noticed a faint smell of stale cigarette smoke in the house, unusual these days, and wondered which of the couple smoked. Both of them, perhaps. Beside the television were two school-leaving photos, of a boy and a girl, a little faded, but recent enough to suggest they were the couple's children. Rut was married to an accountant called Thor.

She was sitting on a maroon sofa by the window, and Helgi, facing her, had a view over the leafy Laugardalur valley. The house was so neat and clean that he found himself wondering if they'd tidied up specially for this visit from the police. The only thing that didn't seem to belong in the room was the manuscript of a book, placed right in the middle of the coffee table like a prop in a drawing-room drama.

Rut had asked Magnús if Helgi could meet her at her house rather than her office, explaining that she didn't want to prompt unnecessary questions from her staff.

'There's no reason to be alarmed, you say,' Helgi echoed. 'Rut, could you tell me in more detail what's happened? I know you've spoken to my colleague, Magnús, but I'd like to hear it from you. It goes without saying that we're hoping for the best.'

'Well, it's just that no one's heard from her for more than a week. Of course, I don't talk to her every day – and she doesn't have a mobile phone, which is infuriating.' Rut smiled. 'But we've been close friends for many years, and business associates too, ever since she started writing and decided that I should publish her books.'

'I gather that she's definitely not at home?'

'No. Oh dear, perhaps I should start from the beginning,' Rut said apologetically. 'I tend to get ahead of myself. My husband, Thor, is an old schoolfriend of Elín's. They regularly meet for lunch once a month. It's all arranged well in advance because it's so difficult to get hold of Elín. But she didn't show up when he was expecting her yesterday. Naturally, Thor told me, and I gave Lovísa a bell – she's Elín's best friend. They've known each other since school as well. Lovísa's a lawyer – a judge, actually, or rather she used to be a judge, but she's retired now. The two of them are so close they're pretty much inseparable. They meet once a week, always on a Tuesday, for coffee at Kaffivagninn down by the harbour. Maybe you know it?'

Helgi said he did, though he wasn't actually sure. He'd grown up in Akureyri and spent little time in Reykjavík's cafés, but he made a mental note of the name.

'It's a very cosy place, with picturesque views of the fishing boats. I hear – though I'm sure Lovísa will fill you in better – that the tradition has become even more established since she gave up work. It's a fixture in both their lives. But Lovísa tells me that Elín didn't show up on Tuesday. She didn't want to make a fuss about it, though, as anyone can forget things.' Rut paused for a moment and Helgi seized the opportunity to scribble down some points, though he didn't usually need to refer to notes as he'd always been able to rely on his memory.

'Elín usually tells us or Lovísa if she's going away for any length of time, to the countryside, for example, or abroad.'

Helgi nodded. 'I see,' he said, but privately he was afraid he might have been dragged all the way back to Reykjavík to waste his time on a non-story. A woman in her seventies forgot to go to a lunch and didn't feel like meeting an old friend . . .

'Is it possible she's deliberately disappeared?' he asked.

Rut seemed taken aback by this suggestion and hesitated for so long before answering that the silence became awkward. 'I can't picture her doing that,' she said at last. 'I really can't. Why would she want to?'

'Hard to say, though I can imagine a few reasons. Not that I'm an expert in missing-persons cases,' he said without thinking, then caught the look of displeasure that crossed the publisher's face. She must be wondering what he was doing here if he wasn't an expert in this area.

He added hastily: 'Sometimes people are running away. Trying to escape debts or avoid someone—'

'Elín had no reason to be afraid of anyone,' Rut interrupted, 'and she didn't have any debts. At least, not to the best of my knowledge. She doesn't have any financial worries as she's comfortably off. Her books still sell well, especially abroad. I work hard to promote them here at home too, and sales picked up again a few years ago when German TV began showing a series based on her novels. That kind of thing provides a real boost. She's never had money troubles, she's always been organized about her finances, and the TV series put quite a bit of cash in her pocket, as you can imagine.'

'It was only a theory, just one possibility of many. Maybe she needed some time to herself, for private reasons . . .'

Rut shook her head vehemently.

'Or,' Helgi said, 'perhaps she wanted her name in the news again, to attract publicity. Revive interest in her books—'

'What rubbish,' Rut said, affronted on her author's behalf. 'Honestly, I find that a preposterous idea. Why would she go to those sorts of lengths to attract attention to her books? It would never even cross her mind to try to boost her sales with a tasteless stunt like that.' Rut shook her head. 'Besides, she'd never do that to us, her friends . . . We're genuinely worried about her. She's got nobody else in the world: we're her family.'

'Fair enough,' he said, though he wasn't convinced that his theory had been as far-fetched as the woman was making out. Perhaps Elín's decision had been an unconscious one: a trip to the countryside, to the uninhabited highlands; the feeling of freedom associated with not letting anyone know, the sensation of being missed and simultaneously becoming part of the national conversation. After all, Elín lived in the shadow of her earlier works, in spite of the TV dramas.

Then again, if she missed the old days so much, why didn't she simply pick up her pen again?

'Why did she stop writing?' he asked.

Rut seemed flustered by his question.

'What? Why . . . er . . . I'm not really the right person to answer that. I mean, she's said more than once in interviews that the series was always envisioned as being precisely ten books long.'

'I see. Didn't she give any other explanation for her decision at the time?'

'No. It was ten good – no, ten brilliant – books, and it's generally best to stop while you're at the top of your game. I respected this approach from a writer like Elín, though I won't deny that it would have suited me better as a publisher to have more books.'

'I know my questions probably sound odd to you,' Helgi said. 'But I'm simply trying to get a handle on the situation. And the first thing we need to do is make absolutely sure she really is missing and that it's not all some big misunderstanding—'

Rut interrupted again, raising her voice: 'There is no misunderstanding. Elín has disappeared: it's blindingly obvious. I went round to her house this morning – all three of us have keys, you see – and it was clear that—'

'You, your husband – and Lovísa?'

'Yes.'

'OK.'

'Yes, and I could see immediately that Elín hadn't been home for several days. The newspapers and her post had been piling up.'

Helgi observed that the woman appeared to be on the defensive. As if she was afraid of making a mistake.

'Can you think of any explanation, Rut?'

'I'm sorry?'

'Anything – however far-fetched or seemingly obvious – that might shed light on her disappearance?'

'No,' Rut answered, perhaps a little too quickly. Her hesitation came afterwards. He got the impression that something wasn't being said. 'Something's happened,' Rut went on. 'That's clear to me. People don't just vanish for no reason. I'm glad the police are taking this seriously, but then of course Elín's a public figure and the police can't afford to mess up a case like this.'

'Do you think someone could have harmed her?'

Rut appeared stunned by the question. 'I just can't believe that. No, I'm wondering if she could have gone for a day trip or a weekend away, something like that, to the countryside, maybe to a summer cabin, or that she went for a walk in the mountains, set out to climb Mount Esja – what do I know? – and had a stroke or . . .'

'Did she have a pre-existing condition?'

'No, far from it. That's the problem.'

Helgi nodded.

Rut continued: 'In fact, she was one of the strongest people I've ever met.'

The choice of words, her use of the past tense, gave Helgi a sudden shiver of misgiving.

2005

[hissing]

Elín, you wrote about crimes, about death – is death a subject you give a lot of thought to?

[pause]

Now, you mean? Yes, I suppose so, I probably always have done, but one's attitude to it changes over the years. When I was younger – younger than you – death was purely a concept, an idea, somebody else's problem. I believe that what young people have in common, most of them, is that they don't really believe in death. You feel that, yes, sure, it can get its claws into other people, but there's no proof it'll ever come for you. The whole thing seems abstract.

I suppose that's how it should be when
you're young. Then, when I reached middle
age, around the time I started writing my
crime novels, I gradually became conscious
of my own mortality. It wasn't any one
specific thing that brought it home to
me, I just finally managed to face facts,
and it was an uncomfortable feeling. I
remember thinking to myself, maybe I'll
give it a go, publish a book; maybe I'll
just go ahead and take the plunge. I
felt I had nothing to lose anyway, now
that the consciousness of mortality had
taken up residence in my soul. Life's
like that: one thing leads to another;
but I'm very glad I made the leap and
decided to let people read what I'd
been scribbling. These days, my friends
and contemporaries are increasingly
going the way of all flesh. It's sad,
but not unexpected. An uncomfortable
but salutary reminder. There are times,
though, when I wake up from a dreamless
sleep and briefly experience that old
feeling of immortality, as though I'm
untouchable, exempt from the common human
lot. A moment of certainty, followed by
wishful thinking, before eventually the
consciousness comes back to me. It's fine,
but that short-lived moment of blissful

certainty is like a flashback to my youth,
because I believe we're simultaneously
young and old, children and pensioners.
We're everything we've ever been.

[pause]

Incidentally, I should add that I'm not
thinking of shuffling off this mortal coil
any time soon. I mean to carry on enjoying
life, in my own fashion. Being outdoors
in nature is what makes me happiest these
days, and travelling, from time to time. I
have a constant need to create something
too, get something down on paper, though
it's not necessarily intended for anyone
else's eyes.

**Can I ask what kind of outdoor activities
you enjoy?**
Yes, of course you can ask. Have you
travelled much around your own country?

**I can't really claim to have seen much of
Iceland, no. Though recently I've been
getting into horse riding. It's great fun,
but it's not exactly cheap.**
The highlands, you mustn't miss out on
them. Though you need to treat them
with respect as they're the only real
serial killer we've had in the history

of Iceland, with the exception of Axlar-
Björn in the sixteenth century. So take my
advice: never go alone into the highlands.
That said, there's nothing to beat sitting
on the ground, somewhere in the endless
expanses of the Icelandic wilderness, and
just looking, listening and breathing –
communing with nature.

**It sounds as if you're grateful to have
been born in Iceland?**

[pause]

Is it possible to answer that with
anything other than yes? I don't want
to seem ungrateful, because Iceland has
given me so much, but it's also taken an
awful lot away from me over the years.
So I don't really know how to respond
to your question. It might have been
nice to have been born in the French
countryside, for example; to have grown
up in a warmer place, seen a greater
variety of colours in the landscape, been
more cosmopolitan. Perhaps I'd have sat
at the window of an old chateau – sorry,
but one's invariably rich in this sort
of fantasy – and surveyed my domain,
scenting spring on the wind, or settled
under a spreading oak tree with a book,

and invented my own stories that would
later have been published, perhaps as a
collection of French poetry. Something
along those lines, maybe? Who knows?
I might have had more money, or less,
but that's not the be all and end all.
I've never really worked out what to do
with all my royalties as it is; I hardly
lack for anything. One day maybe you'll
come into more money than you need to
live a comfortable life and then you'll
understand what I'm talking about.

**I find that unlikely, Elín. Journalism's
not exactly a well-paid job.**
Nor is being an author, as a rule. Just
follow your heart, do something you care
about. And remember the importance of
culture. Of course we want to save lives,
build houses, practise science, understand
the world – that's all well and good, but
none of it has any value without culture.
What would be the point of getting up in
the morning, feeding ourselves, working by
day and sleeping at night, if nothing ever
touched your soul? We need fairy tales,
beauty; we need to be able to imagine
that oak tree in the French forest, see
drawings of it, smell the scent of its
leaves through the medium of poetry and

stories, and – most essential of all –
have a good book ready to hand in case
we find that tree in real life and want
to settle down in its shade to read. I
suppose you could say it's all about
snatching moments from eternity.

[hissing]

2012

Thursday, 1 November

The flat in Laugadalur was history; Bergthóra lived there alone these days, though Helgi was still paying the rent. It was a problem he'd have to deal with sooner or later, but he'd kept the fact hidden from Aníta. He'd envisaged letting the contract run its course – there was only a month left on it – then at some point sending Bergthóra a bill for the months when she'd been living there at his expense. He'd heard on the grapevine that she had started seeing someone else, a man who worked at the University Hospital, but he didn't want to know. Bergthóra could be charming on first acquaintance, she came across as loving and impulsive, but that flame would be quickly extinguished as the relationship wore on.

Helgi had rented himself a small flat on Sudurgata in the west of town, in the basement of an attractive red house clad in corrugated iron. Sometimes, when he got home after work, he felt as if he were living in a story. It was all very alien and different to an Akureyri boy like him. In retrospect, Akureyri seemed almost like a village compared to the noise, traffic and crowds of Reykjavík, even though he lived in an area of the capital that was characterized by charming traditional houses. The proximity to the centre of town had its advantages and drawbacks too.

He had settled in very well, all things considered. He'd had to solve the problem of accommodation in a hurry after the powder keg that was his relationship with Bergthóra had finally exploded. For him, this flat didn't represent a future home so much as a temporary solution.

It belonged to a colleague of his in the police, who had offered him reasonable conditions and a special discount on the rent for the first few months in light of the circumstances. Helgi had been planning to find a larger flat in the suburbs, to buy rather than rent, but Aníta's arrival on the scene had complicated things, and now he thought he might have to add her into the equation when it came to finding somewhere to live, though she hadn't officially moved in with him yet.

They got on so well. They could spend their evenings relaxing on the sofa, just chatting, and even enjoy a glass of wine together. Sadly, that hadn't been true of his life with Bergthóra.

He and Aníta had just opened a bottle of red after a long day at work.

Helgi already trusted her more than he had ever trusted Bergthóra and didn't hesitate to discuss his job with her.

He knew she would never betray his confidence and he really appreciated being able to bounce his ideas and theories off someone from outside the police.

His mind was permanently in overdrive, buzzing with speculation about his cases all day and half the evening, except when he could switch off by losing himself in a book. Although he was careful not to be at work, directly or indirectly, the whole time, the truth was that he relished the jobs that were assigned to him and was eager not only to perform them well but to achieve better results than any of his colleagues. He saw himself staying on in CID for the next couple of decades at least, so he was determined to scale the promotional ladder as quickly as possible. When he first joined the police he had still been working on his MA dissertation about the murders at the sanatorium, so he had asked for an extension and planned to focus on finishing it in the new year.

'Should I give Bergthóra a call tomorrow?' he asked. 'I'm serious. We can't have her bothering you at work.'

'Can we talk about something else?' Aníta pleaded, finishing the last mouthful in her glass. Helgi had tried to bring up the subject earlier that evening too, without success. 'By the way, I've never read anything by Elín,' she added.

He replenished their glasses.

'Yes, you should try some more good crime novels,' he said, taking the bait. They could discuss Bergthóra later or just try to forget about the incident.

Aníta didn't share his interest in detective fiction, but he saw that as a challenge rather than a disadvantage. He was hoping he could teach her to appreciate something new and had already lent her several titles from his collection.

Earlier that evening he had gone through his shelves and picked out a handful of novels he was intending to peruse over the next few days, old detective stories dealing with disappearances of one kind or another. It wasn't that he thought the solution to the mystery would be lurking in any of them, he just needed a means of distracting himself when he was under a lot of pressure. The first book from the pile was lying on the sofa beside him now: *The Dragon Murder Case* by S. S. Van Dine.

'Elín was bloody good,' he told Aníta. 'Was, or is – I don't know what to say in the circumstances.'

'What do you think has happened? Any ideas?'

'To be honest, my gut instinct is that she's dead, but I couldn't tell you why.'

'How odd.'

'At other times I think she might have masterminded her own disappearance.'

When he'd first heard that Elín was missing, he'd been immediately reminded of Agatha Christie, who vanished without trace in 1926, just as she had become successful. She had later turned up at an English country hotel in Harrogate, under an assumed name. Christie had only been thirty-six at the time, while Elín was almost twice that age. Christie had recently learnt that her husband was intending to leave her, whereas, at least on the surface, nothing of note seemed to have happened in Elín's life recently. She simply led a quiet existence as a retired bestselling author. Then, all of a sudden, nobody knew where she was.

'It sounds like the sort of thing an artist would con-
trive, staging a disappearance like that,' Aníta said. 'Then
maybe publishing a new book in the autumn?'

'She hadn't ... hasn't ... written anything for many
years. There's no book in the pipeline.'

'Are you sure about that?' Aníta asked teasingly. With
her, smiles and light-heartedness never seemed far from
the surface. She was the complete opposite of Bergthóra
in that respect.

'Quite sure. I've spoken to her publisher. She wouldn't
lie to me, not in a situation like this.'

Aníta shrugged.

'Agatha Christie vanished, only to reappear again,'
Helgi remarked. 'She was a promising young writer at the
time. She'd just published the book that made her into a
star.'

'What happened?'

'She turned up,' Helgi said.

'Where?'

'At a hotel, under an assumed name. She never referred
to it in her autobiography. There are no explanations,
though there have been any number of theories. I think
it's safe to say that it was one of the most famous myster-
ies of the twentieth century.'

'I think it sounds rather fun, being able to disappear,
then pop up again.'

'You could put it like that.'

'What about Elín?' Aníta asked.

Helgi was pleased that she seemed genuinely interested.
Of course, he had to be circumspect when discussing

69

ongoing investigations, but he trusted Aníta. He supposed he'd trusted Bergthóra too, to begin with, but she'd
never been interested enough to ask him about the work
he was engaged in, whether it was his studies or his job.

'I have to say, I think it's unlikely she'll turn up at a
hotel,' Helgi said. 'No, I think there's more to it. Maybe
she intended to disappear for good and never come back.'

'That can't be ruled out.'

'No, you're right about that.'

'This could be a good assignment for you, couldn't it?'
Aníta asked diffidently.

'A good assignment?'

'Prominent, I mean. A big case.'

Of course this had occurred to him, but when it came
to the point he found it distasteful to dwell on that aspect.

'It'll certainly cause a stir – hopefully not straight away,
but soon enough. It would be great to have a few days to
look into things in peace first, though. As I mentioned, I
spoke to her publisher earlier . . .' He paused. 'She didn't
know anything, or . . .'

'Or claimed she didn't,' Aníta finished.

'Exactly. Forensics have examined Elín's house from
top to bottom. I'm going over there tomorrow. There
are no clues, apart from the fact that she doesn't seem to
have been at home for several days. It's all very strange.'

'Was she strong? Healthy, I mean?'

'Yes, I got in touch with her doctor. She was fighting
fit. I'm going to talk to her best friend as well tomorrow.
Her name's Lovísa. She's a judge.'

'Women tell their best friends everything,' Aníta said

with a mischievous grin. Helgi tried not to wonder what she said about him to her female friends. 'You should have spoken to Lovísa before anyone else. Maybe I'd be better at this job than you.'

Laughing, Helgi bent and kissed her.

1965

'Let's forget the gun, shall we?'

'Don't be stupid. You went to all the trouble of getting hold of it, and . . . Do you really think anyone will take us seriously without one?'

'We'll have, you know, masks . . .'

'Balaclavas, yes.'

'I'm sure that'll do. It's not like it's their money; they'll give us what we ask for.'

'Trust me, there has to be some kind of threat.'

'Yes, but I don't feel comfortable about the gun.'

'We've already agreed that I would carry it.'

'It won't be loaded, will it?'

'For God's sake, why not? It has to be loaded, or it's just a bluff.'

'OK, you take the gun, then. And you look out for me.'

'Of course. I'll always look out for you. It'll be fine.'

FRIDAY

2012

Friday, 2 November

'I'm sorry, but I'm afraid I have to ask: was there something going on between you and Elín?'

The look of astonishment on the face of Rut's husband, Thor, said all that was needed. It was obvious that he hadn't been prepared for the question.

'I know it's an uncomfortable thing to ask, but nothing's out of bounds in an investigation of this type.' Helgi spoke with an air of authority, despite his lack of experience in the police.

Thor cleared his throat: 'No. That's the short answer. Of course not. We didn't have that sort of relationship. We were best friends at school and have kept up our friendship ever since. That's why my wife is her publisher. Elín showed me a draft of her first book and gave me permission to take the manuscript to Rut. They were friends at university. We've all known each other a very long time.' He gave the ghost of a smile. 'So that's how it all began, then Elín had her breakthrough, so to speak. Rut's publishing company was small but grew with Elín until it's now one of the largest in the country. I don't suppose it's easy to find a publisher for one's first book, but Elín was lucky to have friends with influence.' He said nothing more for a moment or two, then added: 'An investigation of this type, you said?'

'I'm sorry?' Helgi said.

'In an investigation of this type – but what kind of investigation is it? Are the police withholding information from us? I'm well aware that nothing's been heard from Elín for several days, but that on its own isn't necessarily that remarkable, surely?'

'Oh? Why do you say that?'

'The woman's an artist. She's always been inventive, full of schemes, ever since we were at school. You never knew what she was going to get up to next. We used to have a lot of fun in the old days.'

This description came as something of a surprise to Helgi. Since Elín had emerged on the scene relatively late, he had never pictured her otherwise than as a respectable, even venerable author. She had lived a quiet life to the best of his knowledge, well away from the gossip columns.

'Just friends, never anything else?' Helgi asked, though he'd already had an answer to this question. But he couldn't shake off the feeling that there must be more to Elín and Thor's regular meetings than appeared on the surface.

They were sitting in the cafeteria at Thor's accountancy

office on Sudurlandsbraut. No one had come in while they were talking and Helgi got the impression that the firm wasn't exactly busy. Thor was tall, with thick, grey hair and strongly defined features. He would probably be considered quite handsome even now and must have been very striking in his youth.

'Just friends, yes,' Thor replied, and Helgi thought he could detect a faint change in his voice, a slight tension perhaps.

'What sort of things did you discuss when you met up?'

Thor seemed to mull this over for a while before answering: 'All sorts of things, really. We just talked about life and our day-to-day existence, as friends do.'

'And it was usually just the two of you? At lunch?'

'Yes. Always. I must say, I don't understand what you're trying to imply with these questions.'

'I'm only trying to get a sense of Elín,' Helgi answered.

'Shouldn't we wait a while and see if there's really cause to be worried before you start trying to dig up her secrets?'

Helgi pounced on the word: 'Secrets? You were friends and met up for lunch – that's hardly a sensitive subject, is it?'

Thor shook his head. 'No, but . . . I'm just not sure she'd appreciate questions of that sort. As you can probably tell, I'm positive she's out there somewhere, safe and sound. You could hardly find a quieter soul than Elín is these days. She doesn't travel abroad much any more, she lives alone, reads a lot, has a small circle of close friends and definitely no enemies. She must simply have decided to take a holiday. My wife makes an unnecessary fuss about this sort of thing; she's keen to look out for her authors.'

'How was she the last time you met? Did she seem well balanced?'

'Was she depressed? Is that what you're asking? It sounds to me as if the police think she's killed herself.'

'To tell the truth, I have no idea,' Helgi said, rather more sharply than he intended. 'It's perfectly possible, but let's hope not. I've simply been given the job of asking around about her.'

Thor nodded, looking a little chastened.

'She was very much her usual self, if you want to know.' He paused: 'Though, come to think of it, if anything, I suppose she was unusually upbeat, elated even . . .'

'Elated? What about?'

'I have no idea. About life, perhaps. I didn't give it much thought at the time, not until you asked me just now. Perhaps I'm reading too much into it, but it reminded me . . . well . . .'

'Go ahead.'

'It reminded me of the old days, when she was still writing. She used to have the same sparkle in her eyes then. She always got so much pleasure from writing and being creative. Apart from that, she was planning a walking trip with her friend Lovísa; they used to go on outings into the mountains together.'

'Do you think she could have been considering taking up writing again?'

'I'm quite sure she wasn't. She would have told me.'

'What about her private life? Could she have started a relationship?'

Thor smiled. 'I very much doubt it. And it bothers me a bit that you keep talking about her in the past tense. As far as we know, she's fine. We mustn't give way to pessimism.'

Helgi had the impression that Thor was a man who was used to getting his own way; that he was more accustomed to giving orders than receiving them. He ignored the man's criticism. 'Why do you find it so unlikely that she could have started a relationship?' he asked instead.

'Because she's been single for years. I don't think she knows any other kind of life. And, take it from me, people aren't very willing to change at our age.'

'Have you read all her books?' Helgi asked then.

The question seemed to take Thor by surprise.

'What? Her books? Yes, of course. I could hardly avoid it; I was under pressure from both Elín and my wife, as you can imagine. Crime novels aren't really my thing, though; I would never normally read them. Though I did very much enjoy her series, all ten books.'

'Yes, very accomplished,' Helgi said, by which he mainly meant the opening chapters of Elín's first book that he had reread on the plane. It was such a long time since he had read all her novels that he couldn't remember that much about them. His preference was for golden-age detective stories by British and American authors.

'Have you and Rut been together long?' he asked, changing tack again.

'Since we were at university, not that I can see how that's relevant. Lovísa, Elín and I were at school together, but I met Rut when I had just started a business degree. She was reading Icelandic. Lovísa and Elín studied law, but it didn't suit Elín, so she dropped out. Lovísa finished her law degree, as you know. Although we're very different people, we look out for each other.'

Helgi thought he detected a peculiar emphasis on these words.

2005

[hissing]

Thanks for the tea.
You're welcome. I'm sorry about the delay;
I hope you're not in a hurry.

**Not at all. The main thing is to make a
good job of this interview, at a pace that
suits you.**

[pause]

**Tell me more about the books. What's most
important to you, the story, the plot, the
setting or the characters?**
The characters, they're always number
one. You could say I got stuck with the
two central characters in my series and
ended up spending twenty years in their
company. God, it's hard to say that:

twenty years – it's such a terrifyingly long time. But the two women, my friends, were created in the first book and survived to the bitter end . . .

Where did the characters come from? And the stories?
The characters came from here and there. Often from the deepest recesses of my mind; at other times they were based on people I knew, or even people I'd met only once and didn't actually know anything about – they just caught my imagination. At one time you yourself might have ended up in a book, under a different name, of course. When a writer's around, nobody's safe. My friends were delighted when they heard I'd given up.

What about the stories? Where did you find the inspiration for them?
Often from my imagination, of course, but in some instances they were inspired by true events. By the time you've lived for more than sixty years, you've seen a lot, heard even more, and the truth is often more extraordinary than fiction. So it makes sense to steal from the truth.

**Do you get away with it, with
stealing . . .?**
Don't we all get away with it, at one time
or other? Frankly, you wouldn't believe
what writers get away with.

2012

Friday, 2 November

'It would have been more fun to invite you to my old office down at the District Court, but I don't have access to it any more. I'm supposed to be retired, though I've seldom felt better. Of course, I wasn't allowed to go on working after seventy, but it's extraordinary how often I catch myself on the point of turning into town, in the direction of the court. I just feel I still have it in me.' Lovísa smiled, her eyes twinkling with humour.

Helgi would never have guessed that Lovísa was much more than sixty and he could well believe that she was still bursting with energy. She had a warm manner and reminded him somehow of his mother, different though they were in other respects.

They were sitting in Lovísa's large house in the attractive suburb of Fossvogur, surrounded by paintings. Every inch of the walls seemed to be taken up with art. Helgi's gaze fell on a modern oil painting above the fireplace.

'He's dead; I lost the dear man many years ago now,' Lovísa said, following his gaze. 'My husband, who painted that picture. But he lives on in his art, and in his children and grandchildren. Elín helped me through the grief. I think I can safely say that she's my best friend.'

'You met up regularly, from what I've been told . . .'

'We *meet* up regularly, I prefer to say. Let's be clear about this: I have every confidence that my friend is safe and well.' Lovísa's tone had abruptly changed, acquiring an authoritative ring. Helgi found it easy to picture her in the judge's seat, delivering her verdict on a defendant.

'I can understand why you would feel that,' he said. 'But do you have any evidence for believing it?'

'Apart from wishful thinking, you mean?'

'Well, yes.'

'Nothing tangible, admittedly. I don't know any more than you do. But let's just say I trust my intuition. Elín loved life and she didn't have any enemies. No one goes missing, vanishes into thin air, by accident.'

'Then what do you think has happened?'

'I think she's taken herself off somewhere and that she'll reappear when it suits her. After all, the police haven't issued an appeal for information, so she may not even know that she's been missed. I'm right, I'm sure of it. You mark my words.'

That's wishful thinking speaking, Helgi thought to himself. Aloud, he said: 'All the same, she should have let you know. You meet up every week, don't you?'

'On Tuesdays, yes. At 2 p.m. It's an old tradition of

ours. Actually, more of a rule than a tradition. You're right.'

'Where do you meet?' he asked, though he already knew the answer.

'At Kaffivagninn. It's been there forever, since before Elín and I were born. Imagine! Traditions are very important, you know. We have our coffee and pancakes, and reminisce about the old days.'

Helgi nodded, but before he could say anything in response Lovísa added: 'By the way, talking about cakes, you have to try this.'

She had served a cake with the coffee – an orange cake, she'd said. Helgi couldn't remember eating a cake with that flavour before. He took a mouthful and discovered that it was delicious.

'So, you'd arranged to meet on Tuesday, but she didn't turn up?'

Lovísa hesitated for a second.

'Arranged to meet? Well, not exactly. It's not something we need to formally arrange, we just turn up there every Tuesday at the same time. If something comes up or one of us is away travelling, we let the other know in good time. That's how it works. I expect it's different with you young people nowadays. Everyone so busy rushing around that it's the exception rather than the rule if people keep their scheduled appointments.' Again, that tone. She was used to sitting in judgement over people – quite literally.

'Did you try to get hold of her?'

'Well, she doesn't have a mobile phone, so I waited for

a while. I assumed she'd been delayed, but after half an hour I gave up.'

'Was she a creature of habit?'

'How do you mean?'

'Did she have other regular appointments apart from her Tuesdays at the café with you?'

Again, Lovísa hesitated perceptibly: 'Yes, I suppose you could say that. Of course, I don't keep track of her daily movements, but I know she used to meet our old schoolfriend Thor regularly.'

'Yes, I'm aware of that. When did you last see her?'

'Oh, the week before, obviously.'

'The week before?'

'The previous Tuesday, I mean.'

'Lovísa, could you tell me what you talked about on that occasion?'

She shrugged and closed her eyes. When she opened them again, it seemed to Helgi as if she had aged from one moment to the next and now looked her full seventy years.

'Maybe she wasn't in the best of spirits that day. She was tired – yes, I thought she seemed tired. A bit down, but . . . frankly, I don't feel comfortable talking about my friend's private affairs – she means a lot to me, you know. On the other hand, I do want to help you as far as I can. Do you see my dilemma?'

Nevertheless, Helgi sensed that with a little encouragement she would open up. The self-confidence he'd been so aware of at the beginning had receded somewhat.

'I'll maintain complete confidentiality,' he assured her. 'We need to make a concerted effort to find your friend.'

'Quite, yes. I'm sure you're right. I feel so certain that she's OK. I just can't bear the thought of losing her. My husband's dead, as I mentioned, and there aren't that many people I can talk to any more, people who've known me a long time, who I've known a long time.'

'We'll find her; I'm confident of that too.'

'Anyway, she seemed tired, as I said. I was a little concerned. Not that I've ever felt it was my job to be concerned about Elín; she's always been much stronger than me. Independent, self-confident, honest and determined.'

'In other words, she looked after you, rather than vice versa?'

A slight smile played over Lovísa's lips: 'Well, yes, I sup-. pose you could say that. She looked after me. I'm sorry, I mean she *looks* after me. I'm not going to let myself be sucked into despair. Elín and I will meet again, sooner or later. I'm sure of it.'

'You said she seemed tired, in rather low spirits. Was she, er, depressed, would you say?' Helgi asked, noting that Thor had experienced Elín's mood differently at their last meeting.

Lovísa hesitated again.

'That's not really for me to say. I'm not a doctor or a therapist. I'm just a lawyer – I know how to read texts, not people. Perhaps you're not so far off the mark, though, Helgi. There was a bit of a cloud hanging over her that day, shall we put it like that?'

'Have you any idea why that might have been?'

'No, not really. Although we're friends, close friends, I don't like to pry. We usually have a good time when we meet up for coffee and we try to stick to cheerful topics.'

'Was she busy with anything in particular at the time, that you can remember?'

'No, she's given up work. She's retired, like me. I think she mainly enjoys reading books these days. Just living her life.'

'Does she travel much?' Helgi asked, careful to switch to the present tense.

'Not as much as she used to, but yes, she loves travelling. Though, you know, sometimes I think she holidays in hot countries just so she can read in the sun, rather than do any sightseeing. No doubt it's a pleasant way to spend your time.'

'There are many worse things than reading in the sun.'

Again, Lovísa smiled, but he thought she was beginning to look tired.

'I understand that the two of you were planning a trip to the mountains about a month ago. Where did you go?' he asked, mindful of what Thor had said.

'A trip to the mountains?' Lovísa paused. 'Oh, we just did a little hike close to Reykjavík. We climbed Esja, up to the top and back. There's really nothing to tell.'

'When was that?'

She appeared to be thinking.

'Er, it was two weeks ago. The weekend before we last met up.'

'And was she on good form then?'

'Elín's always on good form in the countryside. The fresh air agrees with her.'

'About Elín's private life . . .'

'Yes . . .'

'She kept it to herself, but . . .'

'*Keeps* it to herself, yes.'

'Nevertheless, I need to try and get a sense of who she was close to.'

'You put it very tactfully, Helgi.'

'Could you tell me something about that side of her life?'

'She's never been married, as you're no doubt aware.'

'Has she been involved with anyone – male or female?'

'I can't be sure, of course.' Lovísa leaned back on the sofa, then forwards, as if she was getting momentum to rise to her feet. Yet she remained sitting. 'I simply don't know how much I should tell you. I know you're investigating this as a missing-persons case – of course, I do understand that. But Elín's my friend; I can't forget my loyalty to her.'

Helgi sighed. 'You know as well as I do that it's your duty to help me.'

'I feel awkward about sharing sensitive secrets with you. You see, I feel in my bones that she's alive. And I don't know whether you can be trusted to keep what I say confidential.'

Her choice of words roused his interest: *sensitive secrets*.

'Is there something in her personal life that, well, that she believes wouldn't stand the light of day?'

Once again, Lovísa hesitated.

'No, not really. I think maybe you misunderstand me.'

'How can I misunderstand you when you haven't told me anything?'

Lovísa smiled. 'You've got a point. No doubt she's had lovers from time to time, without necessarily sharing the fact with me. On the other hand – and this is something I don't want to see in any police file—' She broke off and regarded Helgi in silence.

'OK, we'll keep this between ourselves for now,' he said reluctantly.

'You must promise me that. I'm only telling you this in case it can help Elín, but you mustn't quote me. Least of all to them.'

'Them?'

'Rut and Thor.'

Helgi drew his brows together and leaned forwards in his seat.

'Is she having an affair with Thor?'

'Goodness me, no. But they knew each other first – Elín and Thor. They were together for a while before Rut arrived on the scene.'

'Elín and Thor?'

'Yes.'

'How long for?'

'Several months, when we were at school.'

'And Rut doesn't know?'

'No. And it must stay that way. I don't think she'd ever get over the news. Thor means the world to her. She could never bear to share him with another woman, even if it was all in the past.'

So, one thing was clear, then: Thor had lied to Helgi, at least once.

'You studied law together, I gather, you and Elín . . .'

'Yes.'

'Did Elín finish her law degree?' he asked, although he already knew the answer.

'No, it wasn't for her. She dropped out in her fourth year.'

'Did she study something else?'

'She worked in a school for a while, then went to teacher training college. After that she was a teacher for many years, as you probably know.'

'Yes. And then she started writing.'

'That's correct.'

Helgi was still trying to process the news about Elín and Thor.

'Thank you for the cake,' he said, then added cautiously: 'I'm afraid I'll have to talk to Thor about this.'

Lovísa didn't react.

'I'll have to ask him about their relationship, I hope you understand that.'

'It was nothing, Helgi. They simply knew each other when they were young, they dated for a short time, then Rut came along. Please, for my sake, leave it alone.'

Helgi gave her a friendly smile.

'Well, we'll see.'

He had the feeling it was going to be a long day.

2012

Friday, 2 November

The winter Helgi had experienced up north had now begun to show its claws to the inhabitants of the south-west. If the thermometer in the car was to be believed, it was around freezing, but with the bitter northerly that was blowing, the real temperature was probably far colder.

He had trouble locating Elín's house in Mosfellsbær, the small town about twenty minutes' drive north of Reykjavík, close to the brooding hulk of Mount Esja. It didn't help that she seemed to live on the edge of the settlement, in an area where he hadn't expected to find any houses. It wasn't quite as far out into the countryside as Gljúfrasteinn, the former home of the writer Halldór Laxness, but Helgi found himself dwelling on thoughts of Iceland's Nobel laureate as he drove, since this was very much Laxness's old stamping ground.

Elín's home turned out to be a detached house, almost entirely camouflaged from the road by trees.

Helgi's colleagues had already conducted a thorough search of the property, looking for any clues to Elín's whereabouts, but so far nothing useful had emerged from it. Today, Helgi would have a chance to explore the house on his own and breathe in the atmosphere of literary creativity.

The walls were lined with bookshelves, on which Elín's own novels had a prominent place, in various languages, but not, apparently, in any particular order.

Helgi lingered for a long time in front of the shelves, scanning the titles. In his view, books told you a lot about their owners, and this collection clearly wasn't one of those chosen purely for decorative purposes. He sensed, and could see from the evidence of the creased spines and worn covers, that these books had been read. Crime fiction occupied much of the space, as in his own library, and although he had never been a big fan of Elín's work, it felt like a privilege to pass through the wall that separated the author from her readers. He saw Nordic, British and American crime novels, mostly in the original languages. And in the far corner of one bookcase he spotted a clutch of familiar titles: Icelandic translations of Agatha Christie, some of them vintage – rare titles that Helgi owned copies of himself but which were hard to come by these days – as well as some modern translations and a recent crime novel that Helgi had heard of, by the translator of some of the Christies. He was tempted to take one or two of these down from the shelves, just to flick through the pages, but he controlled the impulse. He had come here to take a look around as part of the investigation, not to root about in Elín's possessions.

This was the heart of the house, he assumed, though he was fairly sure that Elín had written her books in a different room.

He found the study upstairs. There was a handsome oak desk by the window and a leather office chair. The walls were painted in dark shades, perhaps to evoke the murky atmosphere that characterized Elín's stories. There were no bookshelves in here. Instead, the walls were hung with beautiful Kjarval drawings. The only volume on display was the dog-eared Icelandic dictionary on the desk. There was also a large assortment of pens. This was where Elín had handwritten her bestsellers. Helgi peered into the drawers of the desk but couldn't find anything of interest, just bills and other admin-related papers, as well as a few notebooks filled with indecipherable scribblings. He could take a closer look at them later, if necessary. On the corner of the desk lay an envelope that looked as if it contained a birthday card. Helgi yielded to the temptation to open it. Elín hadn't yet written the name of the recipient on the front; inside, there were two tickets to a football match in London.

The bedroom was clean and tidy, and the bed had been made, though Elín would probably have done that anyway, regardless of whether she had been intending to leave the house for a longer or shorter time. His general impression was of a house whose owner had not intended to leave for good. It was a living home, with newspapers

99

and glasses on the kitchen table, half-read books beside the bed, and a Kjarval drawing propped up on the floor in the hall, presumably a recent addition to the collection which Elín hadn't got round to hanging.

Yet Elín might never come home. In which case the house would remain exactly as it was, and nothing would be touched until a relative or friend took on the job of handling her estate. And no more novels would be written at that trusty desk.

He felt the weight of his responsibility; it was up to him to solve this mystery, which could be a matter of life and death. Up to him to ensure that the depressing prospect didn't become a reality.

All at once, he felt an urgent need to get out of the house; he felt oppressed in here, even among all the books. They would have to go to a new home, he found himself inadvertently thinking, though of course that wasn't the main priority.

He hastened outside into the wintry weather. Not only was it freezing out there, but dusk had stolen up on him, cloaking the landscape in shadow. Perhaps he had been ambushed by this alien feeling of pessimism because daylight had fled during the short time he was in Elín's house.

For a while he just stood there, the door closed behind him, breathing in the icy air and watching the twilight dissolve into night. There were times, like now, when he felt he wasn't cut out for this job. There was too much tragedy involved. It was the puzzles he loved, the challenge of working out patterns that eluded other people, of piecing together facts, intuitions and clues. Indeed, it struck him that the aspects of being a detective that appealed to him most were the very things he was seeking in his beloved whodunnits.

Yes, maybe the whole thing was a mistake and he was in the wrong line of work.

1976

'I'm not happy about this.'

Hulda felt a knot of anxiety tightening in her stomach.

She was sitting facing her boss, Hördur. Although sparing with his praise, in practice he had been quite good to her. She preferred having him as a boss to most of the other senior officers in the police, yet she never really knew what he was thinking. Perhaps it was a deliberate strategy on his part, a way of controlling his underlings, or perhaps he was just a bad manager.

For a horrible moment, she believed he was about to give her the sack on the grounds that her performance hadn't been up to scratch, although she knew this wasn't fair. She worked longer hours than almost anyone else in her position and never overlooked anything of importance. 'Don't get lost in the detail,' Hördur had once told her. If anything, she had taken this as praise.

'I'm sorry?' she said now.

'Oh, that's just me, starting in the middle of a thought.

Look, they want us to talk to Einar, at the old penitentiary. The lad who robbed the bank.'

Hulda nodded.

Like most people, she was familiar with the bank
robbery just over ten years previously – the 'big robbery', as it was called – in which a security guard, a man
approaching retirement age, had lost his life. It had
been carried out by two masked men, but the police had
only succeeded in arresting one of them. The Einar in
question hadn't quite been caught red-handed, but as
good as, and he had confessed to the crime after a long
series of interrogations. But he had never shopped his
accomplice, which meant the crime had only ever been
half solved. Einar was currently serving a sixteen-year
prison sentence.

'Why?' Hulda asked. 'I thought he'd been interviewed
repeatedly over the years?'

'He's been a bit under the weather lately. It seems
prison doesn't agree with him. It's a sad story, depressing.
A young man, in his prime, with everything to look forward to, taking a disastrous decision like that. An armed
robbery in Reykjavík – need I say more? Of course, he
didn't mean to hurt anybody – he's claimed that repeatedly, and I believe him – but you can't walk into a bank
with a loaded shotgun and assume that nothing will go
wrong.'

'Under the weather, you said?'

'It's like he's wasting away in there, losing the will to
live. Not that he's tried to take his own life or anything.
But the upshot is that I've been asked to send someone

down to Skólavördustígur to talk to him. Who knows? Maybe he'll be willing to open up at last . . .'

'If he's dying anyway, you mean?' Hulda asked.

'Well, you could say that. Though, of course, we can't be sure. He may still rally. Anyway, I wanted to ask you to take on the job, Hulda. Could you be persuaded to go? I have a feeling it'll be a waste of effort, but it occurred to me that it might surprise him to be confronted by a female officer. An unexpected, novel experience. After all, he's been questioned by any number of men over the years without success. And you've got a way with people. I've been watching you.'

'Thanks.'

'So you'd be willing to do it?'

'Yes, of course.'

2012

Friday, 2 November

'Thor?'

'Yes, who's speaking, please?' The mobile phone connection crackled.

'It's Helgi Reykdal here again, from the police.'

'Mm? Oh, right. Any news? Sorry, I'm in the car.'

'Would you be able to spare me five minutes later? I can come by your office again.'

'Actually, I've just left. I'm on my way to the pool in Laugardalur for a dip in the hot tub. But I can meet you at my house, in a bit over half an hour, perhaps.'

Helgi deliberated. He would prefer to speak to Thor in private, out of earshot of his wife.

'I think it would be better if we met somewhere else.'

'Then why don't you come by the swimming pool? If you only need five minutes, we could take a seat in the foyer.'

'All right, then. See you there.'

*

Helgi found a parking space near the pool and made a dash from the car to the entrance. If anything, the weather was even more perishingly cold than it had been earlier. On days like these he wondered why on earth he'd decided to return to Iceland after finishing his postgrad studies in the UK. Of course, he'd had his reasons at the time. For one thing, he'd wanted to be near his mother after his father died, and, for another, Bergthóra had been offered a good job in Iceland. In practice, though, he didn't actually see much of his mother, since she lived on the other side of the country. Maybe it would make sense to move abroad with Aníta if they could both find suitable work. Anything was possible and, with Aníta at his side, he was starting to realize that everything seemed brighter.

Unable to spot Thor anywhere, Helgi was briefly struck by the wild idea that the accountant might have made a run for it. He smiled at the thought.

Helgi did a circuit of the pool reception area, which smelt strongly of chlorine, and watched members of the public coming and going, thinking that he himself wouldn't dream of venturing outside in this brutal cold in nothing but his swimming trunks.

Finally, he gave up and rang Thor.

'I'm outside, queuing for a hot-dog. I'm nearly at the front.'

Helgi sighed. 'OK, I'll come and find you.'

He braced himself, huddling his coat around him, then stepped outside, where he soon spotted the tall figure placing his order at the window.

'I'm sorry,' Thor said. 'I was famished. Were you looking for me inside?'

'No problem.'

Thor had ordered a hot-dog with nothing but ketchup,
and an apple juice, like a kid attending a swimming lesson
rather than a seventy-year-old accountant.

'Do you mind if we talk here?' Thor asked. He stationed himself at a small standing table nearby.

Helgi nodded, silently cursing the cold. But this would
only take a minute or two and Thor must be feeling the
chill as much as he was.

'I went to see Lovísa after we spoke this morning.'

Thor took a bite of hot-dog, looking at Helgi with his
eyebrows raised enquiringly, as if he had no idea what
was coming next.

'She told me you and Elín used to be an item.'

Finally, a hint of alarm appeared in Thor's eyes.

'Just a minute . . .' he said, wiping his mouth with a
paper napkin. He was transparently buying himself time.

'Correct me if I'm wrong,' Helgi said, 'but I seem to
remember asking you about your relationship this morning and receiving a quite different answer.'

'We . . .' Thor paused. 'What exactly did Lovísa say?'

'Never mind what she said. What do you say, Thor?'

'Well, yes, we went out with each other briefly before I
met my wife.'

'It didn't occur to you to mention this to me?'

Thor looked simultaneously confused, ashamed and
guilty. 'I felt it wasn't really relevant. Elín and I have never
discussed it with Rut, you see. And there was no reason

to drag it out into the daylight now, as far as I could tell. I do hope you understand that.'

'Why didn't your relationship last?'

'I broke up with her when I met Rut, it was as simple as that.'

'How did Elín take it?'

'Not particularly well. We were young and in love, but I think her feelings for me were stronger than mine for her.'

'Did she ever have another relationship of any length?'

Thor seemed to consider.

'You know, I don't think she did.'

Helgi smiled. 'Perhaps she never got over you.'

Thor's expression spoke louder than words. It seemed that Helgi might inadvertently have hit on the truth.

Helgi was glad to get back into the car. Turning the heater on full blast, he set off for home.

As he drove, he switched on the radio. It was the Radio 2 afternoon programme, a well-known politician in conversation with a female presenter. Helgi listened for a while as they discussed a wage dispute between fishing-boat owners and crews, but he was too distracted to take it in. It occurred to him that he himself might soon be sitting in the hot seat at the radio studio, being interviewed about the disappearance of the bestselling author.

He selected Aníta's number on his phone, wanting to hear her voice, but she didn't pick up. Perhaps she was still at work or had gone out for a run, as she did most days.

Most of all, though, he wanted to hear Aníta's cheerful voice and tell her how much he was looking forward to seeing her this evening.

For some unknown reason, Elín had let Thor slip through her fingers long ago, but Helgi had no intention of losing Aníta.

2012

Friday, 2 November

Aníta leapt from the bus just before the doors closed.

She wasn't at her stop yet, but she couldn't stay on board a second longer.

She didn't catch the bus every day, just from time to time, especially in winter, since her little car wasn't very reliable in slippery, snowy conditions. In fact, it had a tendency to break down whatever the weather. Buying a new car was high on her to-do list, but her money always seemed to go on something else. Besides, the bus stopped almost at the end of her road, so it was very practical.

She had been sitting at the back, as usual, and was more than halfway home when she spotted a woman at the front who reminded her uncannily of Bergthóra. Aníta had watched her, waiting for her to look round, and eventually she did. Her gaze was vacant, creepy; it made Aníta's blood run cold as the woman seemed to stare right through her, and in the same instant she'd realized that it was indeed Bergthóra. Perhaps it was a coincidence, perhaps not, but it had been a horribly uncomfortable feeling.

Aníta had sat tight, hoping that Bergthóra wouldn't try to approach her.

At the next bus stop, she had waited, waited . . . then shot to her feet and made a dash for the door, heart pounding.

Once outside on the pavement, reluctant to run, she forced herself to walk slowly away from the bus stop, hoping that Bergthóra hadn't had time to get out.

Then, unable to stop herself, she snatched a look round and saw that the bus had moved off.

Flooded with relief, she paused to catch her breath, standing there without moving for a moment.

Then the bus braked again, for no obvious reason.

Could Bergthóra have asked the driver to stop so she could get off?

Aníta had got out in an industrial estate, far from any residential housing, and it was eerily empty at this time of the evening.

Suddenly she was running for her life, not daring to glance over her shoulder to check if anyone was in pursuit.

2012

Friday, 2 November

'What are you reading?'

The words seemed to hover a long way off on the edge of his consciousness, faint but full of warmth. Helgi didn't immediately react, then stirred and realized he had dozed off on the sofa with the book on his stomach.

He had been dreaming, and his dream stayed with him.

He had been looking at a small gravestone, mossy from many years in a churchyard. In his dream the weather had been still and the inscription had been clear: *Elín S. Jóns-dóttir*. But when he looked back at the stone, the name had changed and the grave was now that of his mother.

The horror of it still clung to him. He did his best to shrug it off. Usually he didn't take much notice of his dreams, but this one had been so sinister.

'What are you reading?' Aníta asked again.

He rubbed his eyes and smiled at her.

'S. S. Van Dine.'

'Never heard of him. Or her?'

'Him. He's long dead, like most of the authors I read.'

'Are you reading it for the second time? Or the third?'

It was a pertinent question. Although they'd only been together a short time, she already knew him well enough to understand that his passion for old whodunnits more often than not involved rereading the same books.

'Yes, sure, I've read it before. It's a great favourite of mine.'

'Can I see?'

He handed her the book.

'*The Dragon Murder Case.*' She opened the dog-eared hardback. It was a first edition, bought a few years ago. 'MCMXXXIII – 1933. A good year?'

'A good year for crime novels.'

'I like this map at the front. It's charming. What does it show, an estate and houses? And here, yes, here's the Dragon Pool. Maybe I'll borrow it when you're done. Why are you rereading it now?'

'Just for fun. It's about a missing-persons case.'

'I see.'

'Like Elín. Well, quite different, actually. It's just that the case is preying on my mind; I can't get a proper handle on it.'

'In what way is it different?'

'What?'

'The case in the book.'

'It's about a man who vanishes, quite literally, in his own swimming pool. He dives in and doesn't reappear. It's an entertaining set-up.'

'Who's the investigator?'

'Philo Vance – a great character.'

'You won't solve Elín's mystery by reading this,' Aníta pointed out. 'At least, I very much doubt it.'

He smiled. Having an opportunity to talk about his old books made him happy and helped to distract him. He felt the strain of shouldering the responsibility for the investigation into Elín's disappearance, even though no one had put him under any real pressure yet. It had all the makings of a big, high-profile case. If it went well, he would earn kudos; if not, the buck would stop with him.

'Elín's mystery?' he asked.

'It's just a manner of speaking.'

'Interesting choice of words, though. You don't think she . . . well . . . could have staged it herself?'

Aníta shrugged.

'Who knows what these authors are capable of?'

On evenings like this, Helgi thought how he would have loved to have a fireplace in the sitting room; it would have been such a perfect complement to the weather, his book and the company. He sat upright and laid the novel aside on the table.

'Do you have to work this weekend?' Aníta asked.

'I'm afraid I do, yes. But I was thinking of cooking this evening. How does that sound to you?'

Aníta smiled.

'Please.' After a pause, she added: 'By the way, have you seen her at all?'

'Who?'

'You know, Bergthóra? Have you seen her recently?'

The question dismayed him. The last thing he wanted was the spectre of his ex intruding on their cosy Friday evening.

'Bergthóra? No.'

Aníta sometimes asked him questions about his previous relationship, quite adroitly, always careful to be polite and considerate, never pushing for answers, but he usually managed to sidestep the subject, if not quite as adroitly. Still, it didn't matter at this stage. No doubt they would be able to discuss it one day, like a lot of other things, but he wasn't ready, not yet. He felt sick at the thought of having to acknowledge the violence, even though he had been the victim, not the perpetrator. He would only start inadvertently wondering whether he could have done something to prevent it, whether things could have turned out differently.

Perhaps their relationship had been doomed from the start and Bergthóra's character flaws had been too serious for it ever to have worked, even though the honeymoon period had been good. There had been heat and passion during those first weeks and months, before everything started to go wrong.

Despite going round and round in his thoughts to convince himself that the violence had been her fault, and hers alone, he couldn't face talking about it to anyone.

He felt guilty, for reasons he didn't understand. Obscurely ashamed too.

The worst part, though, was the dread he felt deep down that his relationship with Aníta might end in disaster. Of course, there was nothing to suggest it would, and Aníta was everything that Bergthóra wasn't. It was simply that, having gone through that horrible ordeal, that maelstrom of destruction, he now saw dangers on every side.

Perhaps that was why he was so desperate to avoid talking to Aníta about Bergthóra, the fear that her name alone was enough to poison things between them.

'Has she been back to your office again?' he asked, suddenly struck by an uneasy suspicion that this might be why she was asking.

'No . . . er . . . no,' Aníta faltered.

She couldn't fool him.

'No, really? Has something happened?'

'It doesn't matter, Helgi. Let's just relax.'

But he could hear the tension in her voice.

'Did she come to your office again?' he demanded.

Aníta shook her head.

'No, it wasn't like that.'

'Did you meet her?'

'Helgi, I know you've got a lot on your plate at the moment. This isn't important. She's quite harmless and, anyway, I may have been mistaken. It doesn't matter.'

'Aníta . . .'

'Look, it was just on the bus, on my way home . . . I was sitting at the back, like I always do, when I saw her – I'm fairly sure it was her – sitting at the front. She didn't approach me, but at one point she turned round and stared at me and it . . . it was so sinister. I panicked a bit, though of course that was irrational of me . . . but . . .'

Helgi felt a surge of resentment and rage, the same

corrosive feelings Bergthóra had so often stirred up in him. He had believed he was free once he had finally taken the step of leaving her, yet it seemed she still had a hold over him. He could have borne it better if she had been harassing him, but she had discovered his weak spot by turning her sights on Aníta.

'Maybe it was just a coincidence,' Aníta said. 'Maybe she just happened to be on the same bus as me – assuming it was actually her—'

Helgi interrupted. 'It'll be OK. I just need to have a word with her.'

Of course it hadn't been a coincidence, he thought. The whole thing had been deliberately staged.

'Should I try talking to her next time – you know, if I run into her again?' Aníta asked, her voice tight with fear but also with determination.

'Better not,' Helgi said quickly. 'Let's not give her the gratification. Like you said, hopefully it was nothing. She's obviously not in a good way.'

'Did she behave like that to you? I remember you saying . . .' Aníta paused. 'I remember you mentioning psychological violence . . .'

'It was difficult, a stressful relationship.'

'In what way? I mean, she didn't lay hands on you or anything?'

Helgi dodged a direct answer to this. 'Let's just say I wasn't happy with her. Look, I don't think we should waste any more time talking about her. Don't let her spoil our evening.'

Yet Bergthóra had succeeded in doing precisely that.

All of a sudden there were three of them in the room, and Bergthóra's brooding presence was anything but welcome.

He would have to speak to her; he couldn't avoid it any longer. But he dreaded the conversation. He needed time to muster the courage, find the right words. The mere thought of it made him break out in a cold sweat.

People disappear all the time, Magnús had said the other day.

Why the hell couldn't Bergthóra just disappear?

2012

Friday night, 2 November

The temperature had dropped below freezing.

Helgi stood on the steps to the basement, gazing up at the sky, at the stars, or at least those that were visible in spite of the light pollution. He had pulled on his coat and trousers. It was past three in the morning, and he hadn't been able to sleep. Sometimes, when work was hectic, when his head was spinning all day, the night brought only a short-lived peace.

But the night also had an indefinable beauty. He felt as though he were alone in the world, and he savoured the feeling precisely because he knew it wasn't true. That knowledge made all the difference. In the warmth indoors was Aníta, the girl who had saved his life, who had offered him the security he needed when he finally managed to break his ties with Bergthóra.

He was so precariously close to being alone in the world. His mother lived nearly 400 kilometres away and was old and unwell; his father was dead; and he had no brothers or sisters, and no children. His friends were few and scattered. He couldn't bear the idea of having to face life alone. Perhaps that was the reason why it had taken him so long to leave the woman who had done her best to wreck his life.

No wonder he sought solace in his books. They meant so much to him. In a fire, he would rescue Aníta first, of course, and then his books. Sometimes he wondered what would happen to them all after he was gone. Would anyone ever care about them the way he did? Did it even matter what became of them when he was no longer around? He found these thoughts so distressing that he tried not to brood on them. Mortality was such a devastating idea that at times he felt there wasn't enough oxygen in the world for him to be able to breathe through it.

Bergthóra's violence had only gradually become apparent.

Good things come to those who wait, his father used to say. Helgi hadn't realized that the same could apply to bad things.

She had shoved him one day in the kitchen. He had lost his balance and bashed into a cupboard, which left him with a large bruise on his side. He could still picture the scene: two empty wine bottles on the table, of which she had drunk the lion's share, as usual. *Are you crazy? You don't think I pushed you deliberately?* That's how it had started. It was all in his head, and she was the victim. Everything twisted around, because she knew how to manipulate the truth. She had done this sort of thing before, he was sure of it, though he hadn't met her ex-boyfriend to ask him. Besides, Helgi would never talk about what had happened. He knew that, and so did Bergthóra. She had found the perfect hiding place in shame – his shame, not hers – and, slowly but surely, she had upped the stakes.

Good things come to those who wait.

In the end, after many other incidents of this kind, she hadn't been able to deny it any longer.

Yes, but so what? I hardly even touched you. And you've done the same yourself.

Only he never had, but that didn't seem to matter. She had controlled the conversation, lying when necessary, denying things whenever she could.

How could she have turned love – if it ever was love? – into such searing, vicious hatred, and why had he let her get away with it?

Not even here, in the cold, under the stars that pre-served the light of ages past, in the night that concealed so many secrets, could he acknowledge his innocence to himself. Instead, he felt that, deep down, he must bear some responsibility for the situation.

Again, his thoughts turned to Aníta.

She was the one who had saved him from the abyss, from his isolation, from sitting alone in the basement flat of the old, red, corrugated-iron-clad house, surrounded by books . . .

nothing but books . . .

unable to breathe.

SATURDAY

Saturday, 3 November

Helgi's detective novels had set their stamp on his office at the police station, the office that used to belong to Hulda.

He had even brought a small bookcase down from Akureyri and filled it with some of his favourite titles.

A few colleagues had remarked that his office had begun to resemble a library, but he chose to take this as praise. After all, it was probably the effect he had been aiming for. Now he could stay on later in the evening than he would have done otherwise, poring over complicated case files, and occasionally pick up a novel to help him switch off for a while.

He had come in on Saturday morning, bringing the next book from his pile to read during his breaks, if he had time. He'd started it several years ago and now meant to carry on from where he'd left off.

Cicely Disappears, the book was called, by Anthony Berkeley. A lovely first edition, acquired somehow by his late father, with an attractive 1920s cover. He was rather enjoying the story, which involved a séance plunged into pitch darkness, and, when the lights came on, the discovery that a girl called Cicely had vanished. Helgi recalled reading that when the story was first serialized, the newspaper it appeared in had held a competition inviting readers to have a go at solving the mystery. Agatha Christie was rumoured to have taken part, unsuccessfully. In fact, none of those who responded had guessed the correct solution.

And now a famous Icelandic author had vanished.

Day three of the investigation had begun.

Helgi sighed.

His eyes strayed to the corner of the office.

There was Hulda's box, the personal items that had belonged to the policewoman who had occupied this office before him. He had never met her – never managed to talk to her. Bizarrely, she seemed to have vanished off the face of the earth at around the same time as he had started his new job.

At first, there had been rumours hinting that she had taken her retirement hard, which was why she wasn't responding to messages or phone calls. But that theory was disproved as the days passed. When nothing was heard from Hulda, her colleagues became concerned. Eventually, a search was launched for her, but the problem was that no one had any idea where to look.

It was well known that she enjoyed hiking in the mountains – just like Elín – although all the indications were that Hulda mainly pursued this hobby through walking groups, rather than on her own. However, the general assumption was that she must have gone for a solo hike, perhaps due to the strain she'd been under recently, and had lost her way or had an accident. It was the most convenient explanation and made it possible to draw a line under her career in the police.

Helgi had attended her memorial service, despite never having met her.

It did strike him as odd, though, that Hulda should have been in the middle of an investigation when she went missing. Although he hadn't known her, judging by the way her colleagues talked about her, she had been utterly dedicated and exceptionally good at her job. Would a person like that really have done a disappearing act – directly or indirectly – without finishing her investigation first, or at least formally handing it over to somebody else? The case seemed to have been wide open, though there were some voices who insisted that Hulda had been on a wild-goose chase, digging around in a matter that had already been satisfactorily solved long before.

Helgi doubted it had been that simple. The two cases – Hulda's disappearance and the investigation she had been working on – roused his interest, and although he already had more than enough to do, he made a mental note to come back to both later. Out of curiosity, he had checked to see who Hulda had been talking to. He'd also heard about the mistakes she'd made, but somehow he got the impression that she had known what she was doing.

He was careful to keep his inquiries under the radar, as

no one had actively asked him to track down his predecessor, but the mystery continued to intrigue him.

So far, though, every avenue had led to a dead end.
There were no solid clues, either in relation to the death
of the girl that Hulda had been investigating, or to the
fate of Hulda herself. Helgi had achieved one thing,
though, which was to make contact with an older man
Hulda had been involved with shortly before she went
missing. His name was Pétur, and they had talked briefly
on the phone, but now – as Helgi contemplated Hulda's
box yet again – he decided that the time had come to go
and meet this Pétur and hand over Hulda's belongings.
He meant to fit this into his busy schedule at some point
in the next few days, perhaps even this weekend. There
was no point putting it off endlessly.

2012

Saturday, 3 November

As the day wore on, it began to snow.

It was the first snow Helgi had seen that winter since leaving Akureyri.

He had stepped out of the office to visit his old neighbourhood of Laugardalur, an area of attractive residential streets close to the centre, known for its beautiful green spaces. Today, though, everything was subtly transformed. It was incredible how the whiteness of the snow could lift one's surroundings on a dark winter's afternoon. Helgi hadn't liked to park directly outside Bergthóra's place, so he had found a space at a discreet distance and walked the last stretch. Halfway there, the heavens had opened.

Oh well, perhaps the snow would provide him with a bit of cover.

He had pictured Bergthóra sitting at the window, keeping an eye on everyone who passed by, but of course she wouldn't be doing that. She had never been that interested in other people. She was much more likely to be in the sitting room, weighing up whether to have another glass of red wine.

He had done it; he had moved out.

They had never actually discussed it, or indeed any other aspect of their break-up. Helgi would rather Bergthóra had left and he had got to keep the flat, but in the event he was the one who had walked out under cover of darkness, taking his most precious possessions – not least his beloved books. He had asked a friend to drop by the following morning and pick up some other objects that were important to him. Inevitably, a lot of other things had been left behind, but that didn't matter. The moment he was out of there, it had felt like being released from prison, and he had sworn to himself that he would never see Bergthóra again if he could possibly avoid it. She had verbally humiliated him and physically attacked him, always when she was drunk. Helgi had put up with it as long as he could – he didn't know why – but he'd finally realized that he'd hit a wall and couldn't go any further. That life couldn't go on like that.

He remembered the police knocking on the door one evening after a noisy row, obviously suspecting that *he* had laid hands on *her*, not vice versa.

The relationship had been so toxic that it had taken him weeks – no, months – to get back on an even keel, and then he'd only been able to do it with Aníta's help.

Yet in spite of his vow to himself, here he was, standing in the falling snow, staring at the house across the street.

There was their old flat, where Bergthóra lived now. A warm glow shone from the windows and he noticed movement inside. It was her. He shrank back. Was he scared? No, and yet . . . suddenly the old poison seemed to be at work inside him again. The painful memories came flooding back thick and fast.

He tried to imagine how the conversation would go.

She would never take a reprimand lying down. She knew how to get under his skin, how to hurt him. He became aware of a vein throbbing in his temple and realized that he would have a headache for the rest of the day. He wasn't frightened exactly, just full of a sick trepidation. He didn't want to encounter her, but he had no choice but to knock on the door. He had already surrendered his key, passing it on to her new boyfriend.

He reminded himself why he was here. Bergthóra had turned up uninvited at Aníta's office, and that in itself was unacceptable. It counted as nothing less than menacing behaviour. No one should be allowed to get away with that sort of thing. Clearly, Bergthóra hadn't laid down her weapons: the incident had been carefully planned.

Aníta gave the appearance of dealing with it well – she was quite a tough cookie – but Helgi wasn't fooled: she'd been shaken. That first stunt of Bergthóra's had been so crazy that the mere thought of it made him burn with rage.

But he had meant to let it go.

Until the incident on the bus.

Of course that had been no coincidence. Of course Bergthóra was stalking Aníta; she knew exactly what she was doing. And the sinister part was that Bergthóra had almost certainly been completely sober on both occasions. It was a cold-blooded, calculated act of revenge, or hatred, or both. Her target was obviously him, not Aníta. She intended to go on making his life unbearable, poisoning the very air until he was struggling to breathe.

Helgi wasn't cold, despite the thickly falling snow; not yet, anyway. The air was scintillatingly fresh, reminding him that Advent was just around the corner. Although the day was dark, there was beauty in the softly falling snow in the streetlights. The horror wasn't out here, it was lurking indoors, in Bergthóra's shadow.

What the hell was he supposed to say to her?

He drew a deep breath and glanced quickly both ways, though there was no traffic, before crossing the road. He was the only person around, and, looking over his shoulder, he saw that he had left a trail of footprints in the snow, leading to this door. Here he was out of sight – she couldn't see him from the windows – and this gave him a temporary breathing space. But he had a nasty feeling he'd seen the curtains twitching in the upstairs flat: could the neighbour have spotted his approach? He remembered how the man had reported him to the police after a particularly bad argument with Bergthóra.

What was he going to say to Bergthóra?

How could he express his anger in words? Would it make any sort of impression on her? Would she react verbally or with her fists?

Underneath, he knew that the correct response was to go to the police. Make a formal complaint.

There had been two incidents now, and it was vital that they should be properly reported. Then the police could go round and speak to her, without Helgi having to be there. Yes, that would have been the sensible reaction. He ought to trust the system, given that he was part of it, and from his training he knew that it never paid to get into an altercation with a violent individual. Yet he hadn't done the sensible thing, not yet. Deep down, he knew why. The complaint would have to be accompanied by detailed descriptions of Bergthóra's previous behaviour; only then could he provide proper proof that the police might need to intervene. But Helgi simply couldn't face it, even if it was a matter of life and death; couldn't face sitting down in front of one of his colleagues to explain how he, a fit young police officer, had been subjected to domestic violence, then driven from his home by his girlfriend.

He was ashamed of the fact.

And ashamed of his shame.

That was why he was standing here in the snow, trying to muster the courage to knock on the door. And, if he was honest, he did want a chance to vent his rage too.

Things couldn't go on like this. Bergthóra had to leave Aníta in peace – and Helgi too. They had only been registered as cohabiting, they weren't married, and now they were separated for good. No special financial settlement was required; all they had to do was balance the final payments on the flat. The rental agreement was in his name, but it had taken him a long time to do anything about the situation, at which point he had realized that the contract had only six months left to run. That time was now coming to an end and Bergthóra would have to move out, unless she had taken the initiative and renewed the contract herself. They had taken it in turns to pay the rent ever since he left. Helgi had been digging into his savings to cover the payments. Bergthóra would have to reimburse him eventually, but he hadn't come here to call in his debts. That could wait. Besides, he doubted Bergthóra would ever pay him back in full or that he would have the willpower to chase her for the money.

He was still standing at the door.

1976

Claustrophobia struck the instant Hulda entered the old stone prison building, known as 'the penitentiary', on Skólavördustígur; that horrible sense of suffocation that she never told anyone about. She didn't even need to see the cramped cells; the thought alone was enough to rob her of her breath. It didn't help that the building was so drab and cheerless, though it had a sizeable yard hidden away behind its high stone walls. She had regular business there, and always dreaded it, though she tried to put on a brave face. A good police officer didn't show any signs of weakness, she knew that.

She presented herself at reception.

'I'm here to see Einar Másson. My name's Hulda Hermannsdóttir.'

The giant who received her, an old misogynist nearing retirement, knew perfectly well who she was but always faked ignorance. To counter this, she had developed the habit of announcing her name loud and clear every time she arrived.

'Sign here.' He showed her into the interview room, where she was kept waiting what felt like an unnecessarily long time for Einar.

She had never met him before, though of course she had read the news about the bank robbery when it happened. No one could come up with a satisfactory explanation for why a promising youth like him should have gone so badly astray. It was as if one day he'd simply had the idea of robbing a bank – to see if he could get away with it. Admittedly, security at Reykjavík's banks had been pretty lax in those days, and, truth be told, it hadn't improved much in the intervening years, although the robbery should have been a wake-up call. Given the situation at the time, Einar could probably have got away scot-free. The robbery had been well organized and timed, but the robbers hadn't anticipated the possibility that one of the employees might resist – it turned out that an older man had been entrusted with the job of security guard alongside his duties as cashier. During the struggle, a shot had been fired and the man had been killed instantly.

The door opened to admit a man in handcuffs, currently serving the eleventh year of his sentence. He was thirty-four, yet he looked closer to sixty, his face heavily lined, dark circles under his eyes, his hands bony, his hair thinning, his eyes like those of a dead man. Any spark of life extinguished.

'Hello, Einar. My name's Hulda.'

He barely responded. She pulled out a chair for him.

'I work for the police.'

'I thought you might,' he said in a low voice.

Hulda was aware that Einar must soon be coming up for parole but, seeing him now, she was afraid he wouldn't last that long. The poor man looked terrible.

'I just wanted to have a chat with you about that business back in '65.'

'The bank robbery, you mean? Isn't it best to call it by its name?'

'Yes, you're right.'

'I've said everything that needs to be said. God help me, I have nothing more to say, Hulda. Your name is Hulda, isn't it?'

'Yes.'

She didn't add anything, just waited patiently.

'I made my confession a long time ago and asked for forgiveness.' His voice was hoarse, his breathing worryingly shallow and rapid. 'I'll never be forgiven, I know that. I can't even forgive myself. One mistake, you know? One mistake that can never be undone. You and me might have been friends today, Hulda, if I'd finished my studies and gone out into the world, as intended. You're not much younger than me, are you?'

'I'll be thirty next year.' Actually, she was twenty-eight, but in this job it paid to come across as older than you were.

'I haven't met you before, Hulda.'

'No. Does that make any difference?'

He shrugged.

'Not really. I suspect you're here for the same reason as all your colleagues. Am I right?'

'What did they want?'

'To fish for the name of my accomplice.'

'I gather they didn't have much luck in getting that information.'

'Are you going to ask me the same thing?'

'No, I'm not.'

That gave Einar pause. A hint of curiosity entered his dull eyes.

'I want to know *why* you did it,' Hulda asked in a level voice.

'Would that make any difference?'

'It could make all the difference.'

'It's too late to undo what's done, and, as you can see, I'm at the end of my tether. I can't cope with being locked up inside for another minute; I can't sit here, day in, day out, brooding over my mistakes, over the man who died.'

'Did you shoot him?'

'Do I need to call my lawyer?'

'Einar, your situation can hardly get any worse, but, on the other hand, you might gain some peace of mind by telling the truth.'

This time he burst out laughing, completely wrong-footing Hulda.

'Of course you want to know the same as all the rest. Well played, though, trying to fool me like that.'

'Did you need the money? Or did you do it for kicks? It must have been one or the other.'

'Couldn't it have been a mixture of both? What's life worth without a bit of variety?'

'You can experience variety in your life without killing someone.'

Hulda studied the prisoner. Despite his haggard appearance, his brain was still sharp. Oddly enough, she found herself liking him and felt instinctively that he must have been the victim of circumstance. She even felt the stirrings of sympathy for him, though she knew that was against the rules. As a representative of the law, it was her duty to stay impartial.

'Of course. Look, I didn't wake up one morning and decide, today, I'm going to shoot someone. But I think you already understand that. And, you know . . .' He broke off for a moment. 'Do you know what, Hulda? I think you're convinced I've reached the end of the road, that I'm dying, and you're hoping for a death-bed confession. Well, I'm going to have to disappoint you there. I'm not saying another word about it: the case is closed and I abandoned all hope long ago. But I reckon I've got a bit of time left. I haven't been feeling too well recently, but not every day's the same. I'm in no hurry to leave this world. There's no urgency.'

It was plain that Einar had no intention of saying anything, and perhaps he did have a bit of time left. His will to live might yet prove stronger than his body. Meanwhile, Hulda was finding it increasingly hard to handle her claustrophobia, although, unlike Einar, she had the power to decide when she wanted to leave. The mere thought of a prison cell and being deprived of her liberty filled her with panic and she was grateful that she had always managed to stay on the right side of the law.

'All right, that'll do for now, Einar,' she said, but saw at once from his expression that he didn't want her to leave.

That he craved company. In spite of this, he didn't say anything or betray any other signs of weakness.

'I may look in on you again. Please let me know if you ever have anything you want to share with me.'

'I find it unlikely,' he said. 'But I've enjoyed talking to you.'

'Likewise,' she said. She walked out of the interview room, trying not to run, and emerged into the sunlight.

Sometimes she wondered if she was really cut out for this job.

Then again, she reminded herself that she was better at it than most of her colleagues, and that was why she had no intention of quitting. But, for now, all she could think about was getting home to Jón and little Dimma.

2012

Saturday, 3 November

'Let me get this right – you're saying you can't get hold of her?'

The man in the polo-neck jumper seated opposite Helgi was tall, with a long face and an almost totally bald head. He was holding a brimming mug but still hadn't taken a sip of his coffee, perhaps for fear of spilling it on his cream-coloured trousers. His face was a picture of surprise, his eyes almost starting out of his head, and he punctuated his words with a heavy sigh.

'No one's seen or heard from her for over a week,' Helgi replied.

He had managed to pull himself together and shrug off the discomfort he had felt earlier that afternoon.

'Well I never. This is news to me. Is it a police matter? I haven't read anything about it in the papers. I mean, I'm sure I wouldn't have failed to notice.'

'Orri, you're closely related to Elín, aren't you?'

The man nodded. A brief background check had established that he lectured in philosophy at the University of Iceland, a post he'd held for several years. He was around Helgi's own age, or perhaps a few years older.

'She doesn't have any closer relatives than me, at any rate. My grandfather was Elín's paternal uncle and the families used to see a lot of each other. They both lived in the west end of town. My grandfather owned an elegant villa on the seafront on Ægisída, sadly no longer in the family, and Elín lived with her parents in a block of flats on Vídimelur. Life was often a bit of a struggle for them, but my grandfather did well; in fact, he raked it in as a lawyer. He had only the one child, my father – who's passed away too – and my parents only had me. And Elín is an only child, as you know, and has no children of her own. So it's not a big family, as you can hear.'

They were sitting at an uncomfortable little table in the cafeteria in Oddi, the social sciences building. There were students milling around, but none appeared to be paying them any attention.

'When did you last hear from her?' Helgi asked.

Orri paused to deliberate, for an unnecessarily long time, Helgi thought. Was he really struggling to recall the last time they'd been in touch or was he trying to make up a cover story? No doubt Helgi was being over-suspicious, but then he never took anything for granted in this job. It was safest to assume that everyone had something to hide, since that did generally turn out to be the case. Even bald university lecturers in polo-neck jumpers had their secrets.

'Um, it must have been some time in the autumn, I

can't remember exactly when. Hang on a minute, yes, she rang me back in September, on the anniversary of Grandad's death. She did that pretty much every year. Used to look out for me, as none of the older generation are left now, apart from her. You see, Elín was very fond of the old man – my grandad. She admired him. I remember her telling me once that she'd originally meant to become a lawyer like him, but then found that teaching suited her better. I've sometimes wondered if I didn't become a teacher myself because I had such a good example in Cousin Ella. I was seven or eight when she had her big breakthrough as a writer, so I've always looked up to her, and of course I knew she'd been a teacher before she became an author. These things go in cycles, you see.'

Helgi was beginning to feel as if he was being lectured to. Orri took a brief pause for breath, but before Helgi could get a word in edgeways, the lecturer continued, now with more vehemence:

'Really, you'll have to tell me a bit more than this. I'm not accustomed to getting visits from the police. Has something happened? Is that what you believe? I mean, just because it's been hard to get hold of Ella for a few days . . .'

'We simply don't know, that's why I'm here. May I ask – you may have no idea – but do you think she could have been battling some kind of illness? Or depression?'

'Ella?' Orri shook his head. 'I don't believe that for a minute. Of course, I'm aware that sort of thing isn't always obvious to onlookers, but she was fit as a fiddle, always going on walking trips around the country, whenever the weather was good, whatever the season. Is there any chance she could have got lost in . . .' He broke off abruptly. 'No, impossible.'

'Why?'

'Because she'd never go walking alone, I'm sure of that. She's so careful. She doesn't like taking risks. She loves life, does Ella. Yes. But depressed . . . Maybe I'm overstating it a bit, but there's always been a kind of invisible screen around her, as if she doesn't want to let you come too close, as if she's nursing some secret sorrow that might otherwise come to the surface. But isn't that the case with all poets, all writers? They need a bit of pain in order to create enduring art?'

'You're the philosopher, not me,' Helgi replied.

'Oh, I wouldn't say that. Studying philosophy doesn't automatically make you a philosopher. Listen, should I maybe try calling her?'

Helgi smiled.

'No, what am I talking about?' Orri said. 'Of course, she doesn't have a mobile phone. She's old-fashioned like that. Writes her books by hand and rings people from her landline. Sometimes I don't understand her, but I can't help appreciating that kind of eccentricity.' He belatedly took a sip of his brimming coffee, by some unbelievable feat of dexterity managing to hold his mug so steady that he didn't spill a drop.

'What secret sorrow?' Helgi asked quietly, talking more to himself than Orri, his mind working.

'Sorry?'

'Excuse me. Are you saying that you think your cousin

had a secret? Something that might explain the situation that's arisen?'

'The situation that's arisen, you say. You police don't have much time for sensitivity, do you? You mean, anything that could explain why my cousin has gone missing?'

Helgi nodded, refusing to let Orri rile him.

'I don't believe so. She's had a spotless record for as long as I've known her, has Cousin Ella. I doubt she's ever so much as got a parking ticket, let alone anything more serious. I expect she got any bad stuff out of her system in her books. Isn't it often the way? People write the darkness out of themselves.'

'Do you rate her books?'

'That's a strange question.' The philosopher smiled. 'Yes, I grew up with them, started reading them in my teens. Her stories had a certain charm, but then I wasn't exactly unbiased. My parents were terribly proud to be related to her. For a long time they hoped I would be a writer too. Of course, I'm always writing something – it's in the genes though with me it's more academic articles or reflections of a general nature. No murders in my case.'

Helgi rose to his feet. Elín's cousin could provide no answers to the only question that mattered: Elín's current whereabouts.

But Orri sat fast.

'It'll all land on me, then,' he said reflectively.

'What?'

'All the hassle, if Cousin Ella is dead. That's going to

be quite a tall order – winding up her estate, organizing the funeral. Since I'm her closest relative. To be honest, I've never stopped to think about it before; about the fact that I'll be responsible for helping the nation mourn their favourite writer. Well I never. Still, it can't be helped. Let's just hope the dear woman gets in touch very soon . . .'

'Yes, of course, that's what we both hope.'

'How does it work, by the way?'

'How does what work?'

'Well, I don't quite understand. Is she already presumed dead?'

'Dead?'

'Yes, given that no one's heard from her for a while.'

'Actually, it's not that simple. It can take quite a long time for someone to be officially declared dead.' Helgi tried to remember the time frame – he'd read up on it once. 'Anything up to three years, if my memory is correct, but it can probably be shorter in certain circumstances . . .'

'Three years, you say . . .'

Helgi could have sworn there was a hint of disappointment in Orri's expression.

'I'm sure you'll sort it out – you'll find her, I mean,' the philosopher said after a pause.

'I'm confident of that.'

'It's quite a fortune she's built up, I understand.'

Helgi didn't reply.

'Am I right? Or haven't you looked into that yet? I remember hearing it somewhere – a pretty healthy annual income, way more than your average author. How much do you reckon we're talking about?'

'I really couldn't say. We haven't been focusing on that side of things. It's hardly a priority at this stage.'

'No, no, fair enough. Of course not. The most important thing is that Ella is safe.' Orri stood up at last. 'Although I'm not religious, I'll pray for her.'

2005

[hissing]

Are you ready to continue?
Yes, I think so. Thank you again for your
patience, and for agreeing to do this in
the first place.

**On the contrary, it's my pleasure. It's
wonderful to have the opportunity for
an in-depth conversation with you. A
journalist's work, by the nature of
it, often means we don't get a chance
to dig below the surface of a subject.
Everything has to be ready the same
day, there's no time for news analysis,
no money for . . . Sorry, I'm getting
sidetracked, but you understand.**
I certainly do.

**We can take all the time we need. By the
way, I reread all your books. I'd read
them before, of course, but . . .**
Were you satisfied with them?

**What? Oh, yes, very. Very satisfied. The
first two were the best . . .**
I've spoken so often about those books,
gone over and over them. Sometimes I can't
even remember the characters' names it's
such a long time since I wrote the first
in the series. And I've never read any of
them again.

Why not?
Why? What good would it do? I wrote them;
other people can read them.

**Did you just sit down one day and decide
to write a crime novel?**
I decided to write a novel. I'm not sure I
thought of it as any particular genre, not
to start off with.

A story about loss?
You may have a point there.

Based on personal experience?
Loss isn't quite the right word. To tell
the truth, I don't know what to call it,

I feel I've used all the words so often, but I don't believe you can lose something you've never really had. The story is more about mourning for something that never happened, about grief, if you can grieve for what might have been.

I sometimes got the impression that these ideas were like a leitmotif running throughout the series. Explicitly or implicitly.
Well, I don't know how much effort I should waste on analysing my own books – I'm not sure it's appropriate – but you're not necessarily that far wrong. Stories are about so many things, you know. That's why we write, to tell stories – in answer to your question.

I'd like to return to the personal angle and ask to what extent those first books were based on your own experiences?
It's impossible to draw clear lines between the books and real life.
Of course, I haven't – thank God – experienced all the crimes I wrote about. But the characters, events, settings, emotions, they must all have some basis in reality, mustn't they? No one writes in a vacuum.

Do you have any regrets, Elín?

[pause]

I wasn't actually prepared for that question. But of course the answer is yes. It's obvious, really.

And that regret has found its way into your books?

That's inevitable. As I mentioned before, if you've lost something, or missed out on something, it stays with you. The things you haven't done, no less than those you have. Sometimes I feel as if I've failed, but . . . Well, sometimes I have failed. As everyone does, I suppose. Just to different degrees, if you understand?

Do you regret having stopped after ten books?

Not at all. If I'm to be completely honest, I'm always writing. I've always written, since long before my books were first published, and I can't stop now.

Does it all get put away in a drawer, Elín?

Not always.

Are you going to . . .?

I suggest we come back to that later.

2012

Saturday, 3 November

When the phone rang, Chet Baker was on the record player, quite literally, in the form of an old vinyl LP from Helgi's father's collection. The collection was full of priceless gems, and Helgi treated the records with the same care as he did the old books, so there wasn't a scratch to be seen on any of them.

Aníta was due round any minute. She was in town with friends and had stayed out longer than planned, giving Helgi a welcome opportunity to tidy up the flat and finish his book.

He immediately had a horrible feeling that it was Bergthóra calling him. For a while, he'd kidded himself that she had come to terms with the situation, that their relationship was over and would never be reignited. He had hoped she would go into rehab, but in reality he hadn't a clue how she was doing. He didn't follow her on social media or ask for news of her from their tiny handful of mutual friends.

The fact was, he didn't care what happened to her, he'd rather forget she had ever existed, only now she had forced her way back into his life.

He reached for his phone; the number wasn't one he recognized.

He could feel his dread mounting, the veins throbbing in his head. The ringing went on and on, each ring seeming louder and more importunate than the last, until his heart was racing and he could feel sweat breaking out all over his body. *Hell.*

He answered anyway.

A good police officer is always on duty, his first boss in the police used to say.

'Hello.'

'Is that Helgi?'

A woman's voice, but not Bergthóra's. He caught his breath.

'Helgi, can you hear me? It's Rut.'

He breathed a sigh of relief.

Elín must have turned up, or her publisher would hardly be disturbing him on a Saturday evening.

'Yes, it is. Good to hear from you, Rut. How are you? Is there any news?'

'Not as such, no.'

He was simultaneously disappointed but pleased with this answer. It was a disappointment that Elín was still missing, but, on the other hand, this case could be his chance to really shine in his job.

'You haven't heard from Elín, then?'

'No, I haven't. Have you?'

'No, the investigation is still in its early stages, but don't worry, everything's going in the right direction.'

'Yes, I see.' She allowed a pause to develop. 'I've been talking to my husband, and he reminded me ... or, well ... I don't want to complicate things unnecessarily, it was all a long time ago, but ...'

'Fire away. You never know what details might put us on the trail, Rut.'

In that instant, the doorbell rang. He hadn't given Aníta a key to the flat yet; somehow the subject had never come up, but it could only be a matter of days before he did. Unless it was too big a step for them at this stage.

Again, he heard the echo of his father's voice: *good things come to those who wait ...*

'Just hang on a sec,' he said to Rut, then got up and opened the front door.

Aníta smiled at him, and he smiled back, indicating the phone. She followed him through to the sitting room.

'Sorry, what were you saying, Rut?'

'I don't suppose this will help, but the thing is that I've known Elín for nearly half a century, as you're aware. And she has occasionally disappeared like this before.'

'What?'

Why the hell hadn't Rut mentioned this when they met?

'Yes, three times, to be exact, by my calculation.'

'What are you telling me? That she's done this three times before?'

Out of the corner of his eye, he saw Aníta's gaze widen in surprise.

'Yes, or rather no,' Rut said. 'You're assuming the same

thing has happened this time. But that's not necessarily true . . .'

'Fill me in briefly about what happened, Rut. We can talk about it in more detail tomorrow.'

'Yes, all right.' Another pause. 'The first time was when she dropped out of university, in the middle of winter, in her fourth year, and left town. She didn't tell anyone what she was doing and was uncontactable for months. She just wrote to us – me, Thor and Lovísa – and her parents – explaining that she was trying to find the right direction in life, or words to that effect. And that we weren't to worry about her, though of course we were all worried. But I knew she'd manage. She always lands on her feet, she's the resilient type, though she has that artistic temperament, so you can never really predict what she's going to do next.'

'Do we know what she was up to?'

'Yes, we do now, sort of . . . She moved to Ísafjördur and took a teaching job. Completely out of the blue. She didn't have any family there, didn't know a soul, but got a job teaching young children at the local school. When she came back to Reykjavík, she announced that she was going to become a teacher, that this was where her future lay.'

'Had something happened, some sort of shock or crisis that might have explained her behaviour at the time?'

'No, on the contrary. She was studying law, doing well, her life proceeding as normal, then quite without warning she decided the law wasn't for her. I've still got her letters; I was rereading them earlier. *Rut, I've got to learn how to stand on my own two feet at some point. You, Thor and Lovísa can't always be there to pick up the pieces.* I think she was happy in Ísafjördur, though she never went back there. She has nice things to say about the town, though she's chosen to live close to Reykjavík ever since.'

'You said three times? Has she vanished like this three times in the past?'

'Sorry, perhaps I was putting it a bit over-dramatically, but . . . yes, it's happened three times that I'm aware of. We have to bear in mind, though, that she's always been single, hardly ever had a boyfriend, let alone anything more serious – so perhaps it doesn't seem like such a big deal to her to go away for a while without alerting her friends. Some people find it easy to be alone; others don't.'

'Right,' Helgi said, taking a deep breath.

'She has fewer commitments than most people, and maybe she relishes her freedom.'

'Rut, could you tell me about the other two occasions?'

'Yes, of course. I remember that it happened again when a childhood friend of hers died very suddenly; I think she needed a bit of time to get over it, understandably. She was away for a week, if my memory's correct. She'd gone to a holiday cabin belonging to her union, the Teacher's Union. It was a long time ago, back in the days when it was easier to drop out of circulation for a while. Anyway, you never quite know with these artistic types . . .'

'And the third time?'

'When she wrote her first book, *White Calm*. Do you remember it?'

'Yes, I've read it. Didn't it come out in 1984?'

'Yes, that's right. We lost her for two weeks – she'd gone to a holiday cabin that time as well, to finish the manuscript. She hadn't told anyone she was writing a novel; it came out of nowhere. But this was at the height of summer, so we weren't too worried. I mean, she didn't have any particular duty to keep us informed of her movements. Then she turned up on my doorstep one morning – I still remember that it was a sunny day and a redwing had made its nest by our front door, it was a beautiful summer . . . anyway, sorry, I'm digressing, but she was holding the manuscript, a stack of handwritten pages, and presented it to me, saying: *Is this the sort of thing you might consider publishing?* That's how she put it.'

'Do you think that could be the situation now – that she's just gone on, well, some kind of break?'

'You know, I really, really hope so. But I'm worried. I don't know why.'

'She's not finishing a book, we can be fairly confident of that,' Helgi said. 'And no one has died – have they?'

'Sorry?'

'No one's died recently? A death that could have hit her hard?'

'Oh. No, I don't think so. I'd have known. We share most of our friends.'

'And it's a long time since it last happened, obviously. Nearly thirty years.'

'Exactly. I suppose that's the point. Why on earth would she play that game again now, at seventy? No, it's incomprehensible.'

Helgi went to the record player and turned over the Chet Baker record, almost without being aware he was doing it.

'Let's hope for the best, Rut,' he said after a moment,

glancing at Aníta, who smiled at him again. She was never impatient, not like Bergthóra. 'Can I talk to you tomorrow, Rut? Let's sleep on this, and, needless to say, we hope she'll turn up very soon.'

'Yes. You'll find her, won't you? You'll find her for me.'

'Yes, you can depend on that,' he answered – a little hesitantly, though.

'Sorry, I sometimes feel I never get any time off,' he said to Aníta once he had ended the call.

'Couldn't she have thrown herself into the sea?' Aníta asked.

Helgi was taken aback by the question.

'Elín? What makes you think that?'

Aníta hesitated, then said: 'It just slipped out. You see, my great-uncle, my grandfather's brother, went missing years ago, and in the end they discovered that he'd drowned himself in the sea. He was heavily in debt and I don't know what else. It was all terribly sad.'

It occurred to Helgi that this was the problem. Whoever he discussed the case with would come up with their own explanation, based on experience, news stories or fictional accounts. Because that's how people's minds worked; indirect, tenuous connections giving rise to theories. It was impossible to approach a case – any case – with complete objectivity. There was no such thing as a blank slate.

Helgi was now forced to confront the preconceptions that he himself had unwittingly brought to the case. In the first place, he had immediately thought of Hulda. After all, he sat in her office every day.

Of course, he wasn't getting his hopes up that the key

to Elín's disappearance could be found in Hulda's – the world didn't work that way – but tomorrow morning he meant to get in touch with Pétur, the man Hulda had been seeing. Having a chat with him would break up the routine, get Helgi's mind working, and perhaps bring him one step closer to working out what had become of his predecessor.

I fall in love too easily, he heard Chet Baker sing.

Helgi looked at Aníta.

'I finished that book earlier.' He indicated the copy of *Cicely Disappears*. 'It was a good read.'

Aníta shrugged, as if she didn't really care but was nevertheless pleased that Helgi wanted to share this fact with her. It was all so effortless, their communication, everything they had to say, both spoken and unspoken.

'I ordered pizza on my way home,' she said, almost proudly. 'I thought it was a good idea. Don't you agree?'

He settled down on the sofa, the missing author suddenly relegated to the back of his mind. Hulda hovered like a ghost in the background, a stranger he had never even met. Now Aníta was the be all and end all, and work could wait until tomorrow.

'Would you mind coming over here?' he asked.

'What do you think?'

She snuggled up to him, like an anchor that prevented him from drifting out to sea, into the infinite void.

SUNDAY

2012

Sunday, 4 November

The clouds had parted and the wintry sun cast the odd ray through the sitting-room window at the home of Pétur, the doctor Hulda had been involved with many years after she had lost her husband. Judging by the nameplate on the doorbell, he lived alone in the large house.

Helgi had meant to bring along the box of Hulda's personal items from his office to give to Pétur, but at the last minute he had changed his mind. He wanted to have a rummage through the contents himself first in case there were any clues lurking there.

An impressive oil painting by Kristján Davídsson had greeted him as Pétur showed him into the sitting room.

'Have you been collecting art for long?' Helgi asked, to break the ice.

'It's in the blood, you know. My parents started collecting, and I've continued the tradition, though I stick mainly to the old Icelandic masters. I don't have the same nose for art as my parents did, so I haven't broadened my search. I'm afraid I don't keep up to date with what's happening on the contemporary art scene.'

'Did Hulda appreciate art?'

'We didn't discuss it much,' Pétur said. 'We didn't get a chance. But she appreciated these paintings, I'm glad to say. Especially the Kjarval – she was keen on his work. I rather took it for granted that she would move in here with me. It's lonely rattling around in a big place like this. My wife died, you see. Like Hulda's husband.' After a moment he added reflectively: 'Two lonely souls.'

'Was she lonely, do you think?'

Pétur appeared to consider the question.

'Yes, I think so. Of course, I didn't know her very well, but . . . that said, I probably knew her better than most people did. She didn't have that many friends, but I'm not sure that necessarily means someone's lonely. Mind you, she'd been through an awful lot of hardship in her life and I could see the pain in her eyes at times. She'd lost her husband and her daughter. She didn't talk about them much, though; in fact, she didn't talk about her late husband at all. That struck me as odd.'

'She was on the point of retiring, wasn't she?'

'She was asked to take early retirement. I believe she was upset by that. Her job meant everything to her. Anyway, she and I got on well – I think she appreciated the company. I'm sure we could have had fun together.' There was a note of regret in his voice.

'Her father rang me once, from America,' Helgi said, a little diffidently. 'Did she have much contact with him?'

Pétur seemed non-plussed by this.

'Her father? That can't be right. She never met him. She told me she'd gone to America to try and track him down but that he was already dead by then. He was an American soldier who'd been briefly stationed in Iceland, as far as I could gather.'

The phone call Helgi had received, when he had only just moved into the office, had stayed with him. He remembered the conversation almost word for word. The man had said to tell her that her dad, Robert, had called, and that he'd like to hear from her. He'd said she'd know how to reach him: 'No, there was no doubt about it,' Helgi told Pétur. 'The man who rang me – or rather who rang Hulda's office phone – said he was her father.'

'Well I never – how extraordinary. How can that be possible?' Pétur frowned. 'Unless the man she met while she was over there was actually . . .' He was no longer speaking to Helgi but to himself. 'Could she have been lying to me? Did she perhaps meet him? Or did *he* lie to her . . .'

Helgi didn't say anything for a while, but when he finally felt it was time to break the poignant silence he remarked: 'And nothing has been seen or heard of Hulda since then.'

'No, not after that last evening. Or rather, the next day, when she rang me to postpone a dinner we'd arranged. We were still planning to meet up, though. We had a date, like two giddy schoolkids – that's what it felt like. We were going to climb up Esja together.'

'It's all very strange,' Helgi said; then, worried this

might be misconstrued, he added: 'Her disappearance, I mean.'

Pétur didn't respond to this or appear likely to volunteer anything further on the subject.

'Her disappearance was investigated, up to a point,' Helgi continued eventually. 'I wasn't involved, but I assume they interviewed you . . .'

'Only in a very perfunctory way. I believe there were two reasons for that.' Pétur paused and cleared his throat. 'On the one hand, I suspect her colleagues didn't take the matter as seriously as they should have done. She had no family and wasn't properly appreciated at work. No one missed her.' He was silent for a long moment. 'Except me.'

Although his voice was firm, without a tremor, somehow his strength of feeling shone through.

Helgi allowed the words to hang in the air for a while.

'Two reasons, you said?'

'I'm sorry?'

'You said there were two reasons.'

'Right, yes. The other deciding factor was that everyone seemed convinced she had taken her own life. Gone off into the mountains, not intending to come back.'

'But we know that was wrong, is that what you're saying?'

'Of course it was wrong.' Pétur raised his voice. 'She was planning to meet me. And she most certainly wasn't having suicidal thoughts. Why on earth would she have wanted to kill herself, Helgi?'

Helgi got the impression the question was rhetorical.

'She'd experienced a series of terrible tragedies; her life had been infinitely sad. And although I admit I hadn't known her very long, let me tell you something, Helgi: I don't believe Hulda had ever been happier than she was right before she went missing.'

2012

Sunday, 4 November

'I'm sorry to disturb you, Helgi.'

The woman on the phone didn't introduce herself, but he recognized the slightly arrogant ring to her voice. Yet, in spite of that, he instinctively warmed to Lovísa.

'You're not disturbing me,' he replied, then waited, hoping that there had been a development at last. That the author had knocked on the door of her friend, completely unaware that anyone had been searching for her.

'I have a question, nothing major, but I felt I ought to check with you first.'

'Of course. Go ahead.'

'I'm going to the party of a mutual friend of Elín's and mine, a lawyer who's celebrating his seventieth birthday. Inevitably, there will be other friends and acquaintances . . .'

'And you want to know if it's all right to talk about what's happened.'

'That Elín's missing, yes. There are bound to be questions if she doesn't show up. Well, *when* she doesn't show up. I'm not getting my hopes up that she'll take us all by surprise.'

The news of Elín's disappearance still hadn't got out. It could only be a matter of a few more days, though. Either the story would be leaked or Helgi's superiors in the police would decide to appeal to the public for help.

'Let's hold off on that for a while,' Helgi said. 'Can't you say she's—'

Lovísa interrupted: 'I'll say she's ill. That's the only explanation that could possibly work. Elín would never normally miss a friend's seventieth birthday.'

'Whose birthday is it?'

'A lawyer called Baldur Baldursson. You may have heard of him. He's having a big bash at his house. His parties are famous.'

Helgi recognized the name. Baldur had earned a good reputation as a lawyer and defence counsel. A distinguished and honourable man. He was exactly the sort of person Helgi would have expected Elín and Lovísa to know.

'I'm sorry to ask you to lie, but . . .'

'Don't worry, Helgi. It's a white lie that won't hurt anyone. The main thing is that Elín comes home safe. We're putting our faith in you.'

They said goodbye, but no sooner had Helgi rung off than he remembered the birthday card and envelope he had come across at Elín's house. The tickets to the football game.

Could they have been intended as a present for Baldur? The fact that his seventieth was imminent would have come as no surprise to his friends and he had presumably sent out the invitations well in advance.

Distinguished and honourable, yes, that's how Helgi pictured the lawyer, and it now occurred to him that it might be safe to confide in him about what had happened.

It wouldn't take long to find the address, and after that Helgi intended to invite himself to the birthday party, armed with a card and gift.

Baldur Baldursson lived in a handsome detached house in picturesque Thingholt, in the old part of the city. It was surrounded by a large garden, the branches of the stately trees now laden with snow. The noise of the party carried out to the pavement, a roar of conversation interspersed with music, and the house appeared to be full of people. A few guests were even standing outside in the icy wind, smoking.

Although Helgi wasn't wearing a suit, he was neatly dressed. He strode confidently towards the front door. The key to success as a gatecrasher was never to hesitate but to behave as though you belonged there. He nodded politely to the smokers and received a few smiles in return.

Once he got inside he had trouble squeezing through the throng, hardly knowing where he should be heading, such was the crush.

He recognized the odd face here and there, but none of these people were part of his own social circle. They were prominent society or media figures, including a few people from the arts world. He hoped he would bump into the host before he saw Lovísa, as he didn't relish the thought of having to explain his presence to her.

Helgi could never hope to own a home like this. The house was very large, an old, established villa, with elegant, stylish furniture and priceless art on the walls. All of a sudden, someone tapped a glass and a sort of silence spread gradually through the crowd, though not everyone stopped their gossiping.

A woman who must have been around the same age as the host took the floor.

'I know the speeches are over, but we're all aware that Baldur's a huge fan of the band the Studmenn, and we've managed to twist Jakob Frímann's arm to come and play a few songs on the piano, which I know we'll all enjoy. So please put your hands together to welcome him.'

The musician sat down at the grand piano to applause from the guests, and it was then that Helgi spotted the man whose birthday it was.

Baldur squeezed through the crowd and took up position by the piano, as if intending to sing along. He didn't, but Helgi resigned himself to having to listen to three well-known hits by a band that had been formed before he was born, and one encore, followed by the inevitable 'Happy Birthday' at the end.

Helgi felt he didn't belong here, and indeed he didn't. After this brief glimpse into the world of the rich and famous, he doubted he would be interested in getting to know it any better.

In that instant he caught sight of Lovísa and saw that

she had clocked him too. Unable to hide a look of astonishment, she made a beeline for him. She was holding a
glass of champagne and, to his surprise, she managed to
navigate through the room without spilling so much as a
drop on the other guests.

'Helgi? What on earth are you doing here? Were you
looking for me? Have you found Elín?' she said in a rush
before he had a chance to answer.

He shook his head.

'No, I just wanted to meet Baldur.'

'Oh? Why?'

'I've got something for him. Are you and your friends
in the habit of giving each other expensive presents?'

'No, not at all. I only brought flowers. Why do
you ask?'

'Could you introduce me to him?'

Lovísa looked a little flustered. The former judge had
seemed much more self-assured the first time they met.

'Er, yes, of course.'

She scanned the room.

'There he is. Come on.' The firmness had returned
to her voice. Helgi got the feeling yet again that Lovísa
wasn't the type to let herself be disconcerted for long.

Baldur was tall, with thick grey hair and unusually
large glasses. He wore a pale grey suit that appeared to be
bespoke, and a dark blue tie.

'Baldur, do you have a moment? There's someone I'd
like you to meet.'

Baldur looked at Lovísa, then at Helgi, and for a
second Helgi was afraid the lawyer would misinterpret

the situation and think that Lovísa was bringing her new toyboy to meet him.

But Lovísa quickly prevented any misunderstanding.

'This is Helgi Reykdal, from the police. He was hoping for a quick word with you.'

'From the police? Has something happened?' Baldur studied Helgi owlishly through his outsize glasses.

'Nothing serious,' Helgi assured him, though it was a claim he couldn't really justify. 'Is there somewhere we could maybe have a quiet chat, just for a couple of minutes?'

'Yes, of course.'

Baldur showed him the way, and at first it looked as if Lovísa meant to come too, but then she changed her mind.

'My study is in here,' Baldur said, opening a door and switching on the light.

Yet again the setting was very different from what Helgi was used to. His late father used to have a study at home in Akureyri. It had been lined with books, like Baldur's study, but here somehow the effect seemed more contrived. The shelves were made of beautiful wood, most of the books were leatherbound, the lighting was perfect, there was a handsome armchair and an antique desk, all in the same style.

'Obviously, I have only a limited amount of time. Helgi Reykdal, is that right?'

'Yes. It relates to your friend, Elín.'

'Elín? Has something happened? She's at home ill; she couldn't come to my party.'

'That's the point. She's not at home ill. May I talk to you in confidence?'

'I'm a lawyer, my friend. My entire life is spent talking to people in confidence.'

'Elín is missing.'

'Missing?'

'No one's heard from her for nearly two weeks.'

'Good grief. Is this true?'

'I'm afraid so, yes,' Helgi said. 'Have you heard from her at all?'

'No, it's been a while. Of course, I was expecting her to be here this evening. Are the police looking for her? She hasn't been reported missing, has she?'

'Not yet, no.'

'My goodness, I can hardly take this in. Is there any way I can be of help? Naturally, I'll do everything in my power . . .'

Helgi drew the birthday card from his pocket.

'I believe she was intending to give this to you. She hadn't written anything in the card, but it was accompanied by a present.'

'Oh?'

Helgi handed him the card.

The lawyer opened it to reveal the tickets.

'Is that your team, Arsenal?'

'Yes, yes, that's right.'

'Two tickets for a game next year. Very expensive tickets, from what I can see. Were you in the habit of giving each other expensive gifts? Or was there something more behind this?'

'Good God, no, nothing like that. You mustn't misunderstand . . .' Baldur paused to take a deep breath, then continued: 'It wasn't like that at all. Elín and I are just friends. I believe she has only ever had friendships. But the thing is, well . . . I've handled various matters for her, legal business, you know the sort of thing. She had her two friends from the legal world, me and Lovísa. But since Lovísa was a judge for many years, she wasn't in a position to assist Elín with her routine affairs. Naturally, it never entered my head to take payment from Elín for this assistance. I'm not exactly short of money . . .' He surveyed his surroundings as if to demonstrate his affluence by drawing attention to the immaculate walnut shelves and the tooled leather bindings of the books. 'But Elín used to give me generous gifts. I couldn't stop her. So it's more than likely that the tickets and card were intended for me. Perhaps she got in touch with my wife to work out a suitable date when she bought the tickets.'

'What kind of affairs?'

At first Baldur didn't seem to understand Helgi's question, but after a moment he replied: 'Ah, I see. I read over her contracts with foreign publishers, or the most important ones, at least. Naturally she had agents working for her in those days, but she liked to have someone look over the documents for her when large sums were involved. I drew up a will for her as well, and other things like that.'

'When did she make a will?'

Baldur hesitated before answering.

'Naturally, this conversation is confidential, as you mentioned. In which case, I feel there's no harm in your knowing that a will exists – most people make one, after all . . .'

This was yet another illustration of their difference in outlook. Perhaps most people made a will in Baldur's world, in which people owned large houses in the exclusive Thingholt district, but such a thing had never crossed Helgi's mind. His father hadn't made a will either, but then he had only left behind conventional worldly goods, such as a modest property with a mortgage – in addition to the bookshop and its priceless contents, of course.

Baldur hadn't finished: 'However, I'm not sure if it would be appropriate for you to have any further information at this point.'

'So you can't tell me who the beneficiaries are? We must be talking about quite a substantial legacy.'

'I don't have much information about that side of things, though of course she sold an awful lot of books in those twenty years and is no doubt still receiving royalties. But bear in mind that, to the best of our knowledge, Elín is still alive. Which makes this conversation rather premature, don't you think?'

'We're concerned about Elín's safety, which makes it vital to get hold of all the information we can. I hope you understand that? I need to have a sense of the bigger picture.'

'Would you allow me a little time to think it over, Helgi? But right now I need to show my face at my own birthday party. The news you've brought me is deeply concerning and I hope to goodness Elín is all right. Could we meet tomorrow afternoon? By then I'll have had a chance to consult my partners at the practice about just how far we feel we can go.'

'Of course. Thank you for being kind enough to give me your time. I apologize for barging in uninvited like this.'

'No problem at all. Stay on if you'd like; there's more than enough food and champagne.'

'Thank you, but I'm afraid I must run.'

'Can I keep the tickets? To the game?'

'Er, well . . . yes, I suppose so . . .' Helgi said. 'Let's hope you'll have an opportunity to thank Elín in person before too long.'

'I sincerely hope so,' Baldur said warmly. 'I'll see you tomorrow, then. Shall we say at three?'

'Great.'

Helgi paused on his way out of the door and glanced back over his shoulder.

The lawyer was standing very still by his desk, deep in thought. He appeared to have aged considerably on his birthday.

'No crime novels?' Helgi asked with a smile.

'I'm sorry?'

'Don't you have any crime novels in your library?'

Baldur paused, then cast a glance at the surrounding books.

'I prefer to read legal texts, but yes, Elín's books are here. All ten of them. I had them bound in leather so they would fit in better with the rest of my library. I like to have everything tidy around me; nothing too jarringly conspicuous. It's best to live one's life like that, I find, to merge into the crowd.'

1976

The meeting with Einar at the prison continued to haunt Hulda for a long time afterwards.

The despair in his eyes, through which she had nevertheless caught occasional glimpses of his youth; the faint hope in his voice. His face scored with lines long before his time, a young man grey and wan after a decade in the dark.

Hulda had discussed the case a little with Jón over supper without divulging anything particularly confidential. After all, it was common knowledge that Einar was serving a prison sentence for armed robbery and manslaughter.

'How could it happen?' Hulda had asked her husband, but he couldn't provide any answers. Jón was a man of few words, more interested in business, property and the stock market than police matters. He was always so level-headed that she couldn't imagine him ever being guilty of a crime.

Jón praised the food instead. Hulda had poached

haddock, which didn't require any special skill, though it was delicious. As the meal was ending, he had asked – as he did from time to time – whether Hulda wasn't involved in matters that were too distasteful, like meeting condemned criminals in prison, and whether she shouldn't consider a change of career. It was never too late to try something new. Then he had added that one should never forget the victims. Einar had killed a man, causing irreparable damage, and somewhere there must be family members who were still mourning their loss.

Few things got on Hulda's nerves more than comments like these, but she ignored them, as usual. This was typical of Jón, but he didn't really mean it. He would probably be happier if his wife was doing a quieter, safer job, but Hulda had no intention of living her life like that. She wanted to make a difference, break down walls, do something to be remembered by, while also taking care of her family.

She also meant to continue with her mountain-hiking trips, with or without Jón. She loved the highlands and enjoyed keeping fit by walking, but she had the feeling that Jón was losing his enthusiasm for this shared hobby of theirs. Hulda hadn't exactly made many female friends over the years, but no doubt this could be rectified and she could find herself a walking companion. For the moment, though, she was content with Jón and Dimma, and her job.

'I'm going to look in on Dimma,' Hulda said, getting up from the table. The house was quiet and peaceful that evening, as it was most evenings.

She thought about what Jón had said. *Somewhere there must be family members who were still mourning their loss.*

Next morning, Hulda stood in the summer rain outside a block of flats on Kaplaskjólsvegur in the west end of Reykjavík. She pressed the bell marked 'Elísabet Karls-dóttir', introduced herself over the intercom, explaining that she was from the police, and was buzzed in.

'I hope I haven't done anything wrong,' the occupant, a woman of about seventy, said.

'You're Elísabet, aren't you?'

'Yes, I am.'

'Could I have a word with you, just a quick one? And no, you definitely haven't done anything wrong.'

'Come in. No need to take off your shoes. You seem harmless enough.'

Hulda took this as praise.

'There were no women working on the investigation when my husband died,' Elísabet added. 'We can take a seat in the kitchen, if that's all right by you.'

'That's fine.'

The kitchen was small and neat, a relic of the fifties, with white wooden units and yellowish-brown tiles. There was a pleasant smell of fresh coffee in the air.

'I was just having a cup and trying to read my fortune in the grounds. There's more hot coffee in the pot if you'd like some.'

'Yes, please.'

'Has anything new come to light?' Elísabet asked as she poured a cup for Hulda. 'About the robbery?'

'No, I'm afraid not. There's no news, and Einar's still in prison.'

'I was so angry at first,' Elísabet said, inviting Hulda to take a seat at the kitchen table, then joining her. 'But I'm not any longer. You can't go on nursing your anger, it just eats away at you inside. I sometimes take refuge in my faith; that helps. But the worst part is being alone.'

Her words had an extraordinary effect on Hulda, suddenly filling her with a crushing awareness of what it would feel like to be alone in the world. She reminded herself that she had Jón and Dimma, and made a private vow never to be left on her own like this poor widow.

'Will you tell me about your husband?'

Hulda hadn't discussed this visit with anyone, not even with her boss or Jón. She had simply slipped away from the police station for undisclosed reasons.

'Hinrik was . . . oh, such a dear man. That describes him pretty well. We both grew up in the west, in the countryside near Hvanneyri. Our parents knew each other as our farms weren't far apart and we used to play together as children. I never expected to fall in love with him, though.'

'Then later you moved to the city?'

The tragedy felt almost palpable to Hulda as she sat there across the table from Elísabet.

Hulda had felt for Einar when she met him in prison, but she mustn't forget 'the irreparable damage' he had caused, as Jón had put it over supper.

Elísabet must sit at this kitchen table day in, day out, all alone, trying to read the future in her coffee grounds.

But Einar hadn't been the only one responsible; somewhere his accomplice was still walking free, and it had never been satisfactorily proved – except by Einar's confession – who had fired the gun.

'Yes, we both had older siblings who eventually took over our respective farms. Hinrik got a job in a fish factory in Reykjavík, then went to night school. He ended up working in a bank. Have you ever worked in a bank?'

Hulda shook her head.

'It was great. Job security, good pay, a respectable position. He worked his way up; never to the top, mind – he would have had to stay on longer at school for that – but by the end he was an experienced cashier with quite a bit of responsibility. Part of his job was to react to any threats and call the police if necessary. He took this duty seriously – too seriously, the dear man – and fate saw to the rest. I've gone over that day repeatedly in my mind. You see, Hinrik was a bit out of sorts that morning; he had a cold, and I said to him – I remember it so well: *Hinrik, dear, stay in bed today. They'll manage without you.* But he was so conscientious   he'd learnt at home on the farm never to slack – so he put a brave face on it. He enjoyed his job. He'd been at the bank for years and didn't have much time left before he could draw his pension. We'd been looking forward to it, to spending more time together, but sometimes . . .' Her words trailed off.

Hulda was just about to jump in when Elísabet surprised her by continuing: 'Have you found the other man?'

Although Elísabet's voice betrayed how important this

was to her, it was also clear that she wasn't getting her hopes up.

Hulda wished she could give a positive answer, but all she could say was: 'I'm doing my best.'

'Would you like to see a photo of my Hinrik?'

'Yes, please.'

Elísabet got up and quickly returned with a battered photo album.

She opened it.

'This one's the best,' she said, pointing to a black-and-white picture, and Hulda found herself meeting the gaze of a handsome young man wearing a light-coloured suit on a long-ago summer's day.

The man Einar Másson had murdered.

2012

Sunday, 4 November

It was fairly late when Helgi got home. The little sitting room in the basement flat was as snug as ever, but he couldn't help contrasting it with the grand drawing room at Baldur's house. The lawyer's home was testament to a level of affluence that Helgi couldn't see himself ever being able to match. But that was fine, as he didn't actually have any ambitions in that direction. On the other hand, he wanted to move out of this basement the first chance he got, once he was free of the monthly payments on the flat Bergthóra was currently occupying. Though any plans for finding somewhere better would have to wait while he and Aníta were settling into their relationship, because he envisaged taking his next steps on the housing ladder with her. Perhaps she could sell her flat and they could invest in a little terraced house together, somewhere in the suburbs. In time, no doubt, they would become the average Icelandic family, because that's what he dreamt about, not riches and a swanky house in Thingholt. If he had an ambition, it was to make a name for himself in the police and rise up the ranks, and the first step in that process would be to find out what had happened to Elín.

He had a hunch that he was closer to the truth than he knew.

His day hadn't gone quite as planned; first there had been Lovísa's phone call, then he had found himself gate-crashing a birthday party. Now, though, he was ensconced on the sofa with a book he had taken from the shelf that morning but hadn't yet had a chance to start: *A Graveyard to Let* by Carter Dickson, alias John Dickson Carr. Helgi had never read it; indeed, he'd never got on particularly well with Carr's work, as it was very focused on so-called impossible crimes. Other golden-age authors tended to appeal to him more. Nevertheless, he had included this novel in his 'to read' pile at the beginning of the investigation because it centred on a missing-persons case. In fact, the plot wasn't dissimilar to the whodunnit he had just been reading by Van Dine – a man dives into a swimming pool, fully clothed, and vanishes . . .

The trouble was, Helgi was missing Aníta; he had to admit it to himself. She was staying at her place this evening as she had friends visiting and they were likely to stay until late. 'So it's not worth my coming over,' she had told him.

He had rarely experienced this feeling with Bergthóra. He'd looked forward to the evenings when she had been out with her friends – not that she had many – as that had been his opportunity to relax and read. Yet now he found he didn't feel like opening the book in his hand. Perhaps it was the author, perhaps he was too restless – his mind whirring with theories about the two missing women, Elín and Hulda – or perhaps he was just so in love that he couldn't wait to see Aníta again.

The book could wait.

Sometimes it was fine to break with habit and do nothing at all.

He settled down more comfortably on the sofa and closed his eyes, laying the paperback on the table.

He was tired from the events of the day, from his busy week. He would see Aníta again tomorrow.

2012

Sunday, 4 November

Aníta was getting very used to spending her evenings with Helgi at 'the red house', as she called the old corrugated-iron-clad house on Sudurgata. But now she was expecting friends and the plan was to have a fun evening at her place, which was in a low-rise block of flats in the modern suburb of Grafarvogur. The area had been developed in the late 1980s, initially focusing mostly on private houses, rather than flats, although that had changed as the area expanded.

Aníta had lived in Grafarvogur since she was a teenager, first with her parents, then in two different places after she flew the nest, though never far from her family. Now, however, her relationship with Helgi was going so well that the time was approaching when she would be able to cut the umbilical cord and move away. They hadn't discussed the possibility directly yet, proceeding cautiously in everything, but of course it was obvious that the next step would be to buy a flat together. He rented his place but often talked about wanting to get on the property ladder before house prices skyrocketed beyond his means. In general, there was nothing they couldn't discuss, and they got on incredibly well, even though she didn't share his enthusiasm for crime fiction. It seemed there was only one subject that was out of bounds – his relationship with Bergthóra. It was plain from everything he said or omitted to say that it had ended badly, but he seemed to go out of his way to avoid discussing any details. Perhaps he just needed more time, more distance. After all, Aníta had to admit to herself that she didn't talk much about her exes either. Her longest relationship to date had been with a young man who had been so immersed in working for the Independence Party that he had talked about almost nothing but politics. When he had hinted that he was going to stand as a candidate in the next election, she had realized that they didn't have a future together. She had absolutely no interest in being married to a politician. She thought wryly that no doubt she would have said the same of policemen in the past, but, with his nose permanently buried in a book and his reluctance to talk about his job after hours, Helgi wasn't exactly your typical police officer. She often had to prompt him with questions before he would tell her what he had been up to during the day. Yet she got the impression that he was pretty competent.

Yes, she was missing him, though a bit of distance was healthy. She had told him that for once she was going to sleep at her place, but it occurred to her now that she could simply change her mind and take a taxi over to his flat later, after the girls had gone home. She wasn't going to give in to the urge, though, as it was also important to preserve her independence and stick to her plans.

She had cooked a spicy Moroccan chicken tagine for the girls and bought ingredients for a variety of cocktails. It should be a good evening.

Aníta had half an hour or so to relax before the fun began, so she switched on the TV and put a DVD in the player, a film she knew Helgi wouldn't be interested in.

It was easy to picture the future, the two of them together, finding a flat, starting a family. He sometimes whispered to her that he wanted to go back to university, study literature alongside his job, write articles and essays about the crime novels he loved so much. And of course she would support him in that.

She had just made herself comfortable on the sofa when the doorbell rang downstairs.

Few things irritated her more than guests who turned up early; in this instance, way too early. It was probably Rósa; she had no sense of time, though in her case this usually meant she arrived late.

Aníta went over to the doorphone, in no particular hurry.

'Hello?'

'Aníta?'

'Who's that? Is it Rósa?' She didn't recognize the voice, but then the sound quality over the intercom left a lot to be desired.

'It's Bergthóra, Helgi's partner.'

For a moment everything went black. Aníta knew she hadn't misheard, though she wished she had.

'What? Who?' she asked, instead of hanging up.

She could feel her heart rate shooting up, even though there was plenty of distance between them: Bergthóra was standing outside in the cold, while Aníta was safe in her flat. She wasn't actually afraid of this woman, she told herself, but this harassment had to stop.

'Bergthóra, I said. We met at your office. I just wanted a quick word with you, if you could maybe let me in—'

'Certainly not. I've got visitors. Will you please stop—'

'I thought you might want to know—' Bergthóra said, breaking off tantalizingly.

'Know what?' Aníta asked, though her instincts were warning her not to.

'About Helgi. He came to see me yesterday.'

'No, he didn't.'

'Yes, he did. He came by – to tell me off. He said I should leave you alone. We ended up having a row, like in the old days, and you can probably imagine how it ended.'

'How what ended? You're just trying to mess with my head, but I think you should go now and—'

'We slept together. And it was so good, just like it used to be. I expect he forgot to mention the fact to you, didn't he?'

'Stop lying and leave me alone!' Aníta shrieked into the intercom, and hung up.

She sat down on the sofa, drew a shaky breath and tried to come to terms with what had just happened.

That bloody bitch.

Aníta wasn't going to let her ruin the evening.

She wasn't going to tell Helgi about this visit either, not straight away. If anything, she would talk it over with her best friend first.

She leaned back, closed her eyes and tried to get things straight in her head.

Bergthóra was lying, of course.

Of course Helgi hadn't gone to see her, hadn't slept with her . . .

But in spite of her certainty, Bergthóra had managed to sow tiny seeds of doubt in Aníta's mind, and that in itself was unforgivable.

From the *DV* newspaper,
1 November 2004

Who is Marteinn Einarsson?

On 10 November a new crime novel, Killer, *is due out from the pen of Marteinn Einarsson. In it, readers will be able to follow the further adventures of Detective Reimar in 1960s Reykjavík. Marteinn first appeared on the scene in 1995 and a year later he published his first story in the Reimar series. Many of Marteinn's books have been translated into English and have achieved considerable popularity in the UK. Recently, major British newspaper the* Sunday Times *likened the central character Reimar to Ian Rankin's Inspector Rebus. But the biggest mystery associated with the series, and the best-kept secret in Icelandic publishing, is who is hiding behind the pseudonym 'Marteinn Einarsson'. Various names have been put forward, including those of politicians, and some people believe there is more than one individual behind the books. Marteinn's publisher, Rut Thoroddsen, has so far deftly deflected all attempts to find out the truth, saying: 'I'm taking the secret to my grave. Besides, I wouldn't want to deprive the public of an entertaining puzzle.'*

MONDAY

2012

Monday, 5 November

It's like an old summer cabin, only bigger, was Helgi's immediate reaction when he first set foot in Kaffivag-ninn. He instinctively felt at home there and had no difficulty understanding why Lovísa and Elín had chosen this café for their regular meet-ups. The place had a timeless air. It stood right on the harbour, almost at the end of the jetty, as if it might slide off any minute and sail out to sea.

Helgi took in the rustic wood panelling and the linger-ing smell of food in the air. He studied the menu and saw that it offered a number of fish dishes, as you'd expect, but at this hour they were serving breakfast.

Two of the tables were occupied. In a corner by the window, a young man sat with a laptop, absorbed in some task, perhaps writing a story, like Elín. In the middle of the room, there was a table full of men in late middle age, who Helgi thought looked like old fishermen meeting for their morning coffee, as close to the sea as they could get without leaving dry land.

Helgi hadn't come here with any particular purpose in mind. Mostly he just wanted to see the two women's meeting place for himself and to make a few inquiries while he was on the premises.

The young woman behind the counter smiled at him when he approached.

'What can I offer you?'

He took a closer look at the menu and the pastries on offer, lingering over the pancake rolls. They reminded him of his grandmother up north, who had been a dab hand at making them, though somehow her skill hadn't been passed down to the next generation, let alone to his.

'Maybe I'll have a couple of those pancakes,' he said, 'and a cup of coffee.'

He paid for the refreshments, but didn't immediately move away.

'Sorry, but I'm from the police. I couldn't ask you a few questions, could I?' he asked in a low voice.

'What?'

'It's nothing serious, but we're looking into an incident involving two older women who are regulars here.'

'Oh? Well, I don't know . . .'

'They meet here every Tuesday at two. Do you work on Tuesdays?'

'Yes, actually, Monday to Thursday, here behind the counter. There's always someone in the kitchen too.'

Helgi hurriedly trawled through his memory for the dates.

'I gather they were last here on 23 October. Were you working that day?'

The girl thought.

'Er, yes, that's quite recent. I haven't taken any time off since the beginning of September.'

'Their names are Lovísa and Elín. Do you remember them?'

'Hard to say; there are a lot of regulars here.'

'Hang on a sec . . .'

Helgi pulled out his phone and showed her photos, first of Lovísa, then of Elín.

'They seem like they might be familiar, but I'm not very good with faces.'

'This woman is called Elín S. Jónsdóttir.' He showed her the photo again. 'She's a well-known author.'

'Oh yes, I recognize the name. Dad reads her books, but I didn't know what she looked like. As I said, I feel as if I recognize them, but I couldn't tell you when they meet here or how often. I don't mix with the customers much.' She smiled again. 'You can top up your coffee yourself, if you like.'

'Thanks.'

'Just take a seat anywhere. There's plenty of room. You can sit outside too, if it's not too cold for you.'

Helgi decided to risk the cold and stepped outside, where he took in the view of the sea and the boats, and noticed that for once the sun was peeping out from behind the clouds.

He gave thanks for the bright morning.

He could do with a bit of energy and fresh air to help him start the day.

2012

Monday, 5 November

Baldur Baldursson cut as distinguished a figure behind his desk at the law practice as he had at his seventieth-birthday party. His suit today was darker than the one he had worn the previous evening but looked as if it had been made by the same tailor.

'It's a pity you couldn't stay longer yesterday,' was Baldur's opening comment, though it was fairly clear he didn't mean it.

'It was a splendid party. A belated happy birthday, by the way. I'm afraid I completely forgot to say it yesterday, in all the excitement.'

'Thank you. Though all these birthdays tend to merge together by the time you're my age. The years pass so quickly. I didn't actually want to make a big fuss about this one. It was my wife who twisted my arm.' Another lie, Helgi thought, smiling wryly to himself. The lawyer had obviously been in his element at yesterday's champagne reception.

Helgi took a seat as if he were a client, reflecting privately that he was glad he had never needed the services of a lawyer. Even when he sold – and repurchased – his father's bookshop, the contracts had been drawn up on the computer at home, without any specialist knowledge, but they had done the trick.

Helgi got straight to the point: 'Have you had a chance to consult your colleagues?'

Baldur adjusted his glasses on his nose, then said: 'Some of the partners weren't at all happy about the idea; they wanted you to present a warrant.'

Helgi pictured a room full of older men; somehow he couldn't see a woman being part of that gathering.

'Whereas I myself recommended finding a middle way; trying to adopt a course that would satisfy everyone without involving a judge in the matter.'

'I see.'

'I proposed the following solution, which my partners eventually agreed to: that I should show you the will here in my office but that you wouldn't be allowed to take it away with you. And it goes without saying that you would have to maintain complete discretion about its contents.'

Helgi deliberated. The offer was better than nothing, and he didn't want to clash with a man who argued in court for a living.

'That sounds like a good compromise for now. Thank you very much.'

'Right, then. I have the document here.'

Baldur pushed a thin white cardboard folder across the desk, then leaned back in his chair.

Helgi drew the document from the folder and started reading.

The will was more than ten years old. It had been made in 2001.

He was expecting Orri to be named as Elín's sole heir, and indeed his name was one of the first things he spotted. Ten million krónur were to go to her cousin Orri; a generous sum, though Helgi suspected that the author's assets were considerably larger.

All her other assets . . .

All her other assets were to go to Kristín Unnur Árnadóttir.

Helgi did a double-take. He read this sentence twice to be sure he hadn't missed something.

Then he read the rest of the document to the end before raising his eyes to the lawyer.

'Who is she? This Kristín?'

Baldur shrugged.

'You know, Helgi, I haven't the faintest idea.'

There was only one person in the national register with exactly the same name, a forty-six-year-old woman who, as far as Helgi could ascertain, worked as a radio presenter. Perhaps he should have recognized her name.

He took himself over to the Broadcasting Centre on Efstaleiti. It was getting on for 5 p.m., so he wasn't sure he'd catch her, but it was worth a try. He preferred to talk to people face to face if possible, as expressions often gave away more than words.

The Broadcasting Centre had always held a certain

charm for Helgi. As a kid he used to sit by the radio at home in Akureyri, listening with his parents to plays, talk shows and music programmes. In those days he knew the names of the radio presenters, including the newsreaders.

He went up to the older man sitting on reception.

'Kristín Unnur Árnadóttir – I was wondering if I could have a word with her?'

The man looked at the clock.

'She's, er, on air at the moment. Are you here as a guest on her afternoon programme?'

'No, nothing like that. I'm from the police. I just need a very quick word with her.'

'Oh, right, it's like that, is it?' The man couldn't hide his curiosity. 'I'll see if I can find her. Would you like to come with me?'

Helgi followed him into the large inner space, thinking that this was where the enchantment was created. They passed one studio after another. Finally he was invited to take a seat on a sofa in front of one of them.

Shortly afterwards, a woman stepped out of the studio. She was tall with long blonde hair and large eyes. She looked vaguely familiar, he thought, though he couldn't place her. Perhaps she was on television too.

'Hi, I'm Kristín – did you want to talk to me? Are you from the police?'

She seemed a little worried, which was understandable. Receiving a visit from the police was never a comfortable experience.

'Yes, I am. The name's Helgi Reykdal. Could we have

a brief chat?' He glanced at the studio door, then back at her. 'Do you have ten, fifteen minutes to spare?'

She shrugged.

'Not really, not immediately. Would you be able to hang on a bit?'

He smiled, though for once he hadn't thought to bring a book with him.

'Sure, no problem.'

'My programme finishes at six, but I can get away a little earlier. I'll ask my colleague to cover the last quarter of an hour for me.'

The time passed quickly. Helgi fetched himself a coffee, cheekily using a mug labelled with the name of a well-known newsreader.

Kristín reappeared sooner than expected. This time she smiled at him, appearing more relaxed than she had been earlier. Perhaps she had concluded that his reason for wanting to talk to her couldn't be that serious since he was happy to have a coffee and wait for her to finish.

She sat down on a sofa facing him.

'So, what is it you want, Helgi?' Her eyes narrowed, though her face was still friendly. He felt for a moment as if she were interviewing him for the radio.

'I have to admit that I'm here on rather an unusual errand. Are you familiar with the author Elín S. Jóns-dóttir?'

'Aren't we all?'

'Have you ever met?'

'Only once. We don't know each other personally, I think I'm safe in saying. Why do you ask?'

Helgi drew a deep breath.

'What I'm about to tell you should not be public knowledge. I hope you understand what I'm saying?'

'Of course.'

'No one's heard from Elín for some time,' Helgi said in a level voice. 'And we're all concerned for her well-being – the police, her publisher and her friends.'

'Has she gone missing, is that it?'

'You could say that.'

'Dead?'

Helgi hesitated.

'Impossible to tell at this stage.'

'I see. What else would be required?'

'I'm sorry?'

'For her to be declared dead if she doesn't turn up?'

The question was so unexpected that Helgi was completely wrongfooted.

'Hard to say. It would require a court order and, if I remember right, that could take quite a long time. At present . . .'

. . . she's caught in some sort of limbo between life and death, he wanted to say.

'At present she's only being treated as missing.'

'OK. In other words, she could be alive.'

Again, Kristín's reaction took him aback.

She seemed preoccupied, but eventually she continued: 'Sorry, but what has all this got to do with me?'

'I'm looking for someone by the name of Kristín Unnur Árnadóttir. And as far as I can tell, you're the only one in the country.'

'That's right. I've never had an exact namesake.'

'Right. Well, strange as it may sound, your name cropped up in Elín's will.'

'What? Are you serious?'

Her astonishment appeared to be genuine.

'Quite. We can't understand it. You said you didn't know each other?'

'No, I can't really say we did. I met her once, as I mentioned. But only in a professional context.' She lowered her gaze. 'I don't understand it either. I just can't take it in.' Then she added, her eyes sharp again: 'Her will, you said? Why have you been looking at her will if she's still alive?'

'It's not official. We're simply trying to look into all angles. I was hoping her will might shed some light on the matter, and it pointed to you. But our chat seems to have left me with more questions than answers.'

'Then imagine how I feel!' Kristín smiled, but still seemed rather dazed.

And Helgi still hadn't dropped his bombshell.

Picking his words carefully, he said: 'Any discussion of her will is pretty theoretical at this stage, while we don't know what's happened to Elín. If she turns up, alive and well, I'll probably have told you more than she would have wanted.'

Kristín nodded.

'But the situation is that you're pretty much Elín's sole heir.'

Kristín stared at him, not saying a word.

'I realize this must come as a surprise to you,' he said after a lengthy silence.

'You must be joking, surely? I . . . I'm speechless. Are you serious?'

'You can talk to her lawyer, if you like.' Helgi was promising more than he could deliver here, as he wasn't at all sure that Baldur would be willing to confirm anything. 'His name's Baldur Baldursson. And I assure you that this is no joke, Kristín.'

'But why . . . why would she do that?'

'That's the big question. I'm trying to work it out myself.'

Kristín stood up.

'Please excuse me, Helgi, but I need some time to think.'

He rose to his feet as well.

'I understand. Will you get in touch if you think of anything that could be relevant?'

'Of course I will,' she said, avoiding his eye.

After a moment she asked: 'Is it a lot of money?'

'Her legacy?'

'Yes.'

'I can't really say at this stage, but I assume she has considerable assets, yes.'

'OK,' Kristín said. 'Right, OK. Can I call you, then?'

'Yes, please do.'

2012

Monday, 5 November

'Sorry to bother you.'

Rut had rung Helgi late in the evening for the second time in a couple of days. And once again she seemed very agitated.

'That's all right, Rut.'

'Do you have a moment?'

'Yes, go ahead.'

'No, I mean, for a quick meeting?'

'Now? Can't it wait?'

Helgi glanced at Aníta and shrugged. So much for their cosy evening together.

'Not really. I could pop over to yours, or . . .'

Helgi glanced round the room. The flat was fairly tidy, but even so he was keen to avoid a visit from a woman he barely knew.

'Why don't I just come round to yours?' he asked, despite his reluctance to go out in the miserable weather.

The bright morning had soon clouded over and, in typical Reykjavík fashion, it had started to rain, washing away all the snow that had fallen at the weekend.

'I'm already in the car. It's really not a problem. Where do you live?'

He rolled his eyes and gave her his address, then rang off.

'There's, um . . . Look, there's a woman coming round,' he said to Aníta. 'I don't know what she wants.'

'I hope you at least know who she is?' Aníta grinned.

Helgi laughed. 'Yes, I do, actually.' He could feel the tiredness creeping over him after a long day working on the investigation. All he wanted was to lie on the sofa with his book and read for a while or chat to Aníta. Despite not having known each other long, they found it easy to sit together in companionable silence. He appreciated that. 'Her name's Rut. She's Elín's publisher.'

'Ah. It'll be interesting to meet her.'

Bergthóra would never have reacted like that, but then it would never have occurred to him to agree to an unexpected visit if she had been at home. Since they'd split up, it had been slowly dawning on him how reluctant he had been to introduce her to his friends and colleagues. She had sometimes been on her best behaviour around other people, but only when she was sober and in the right mood.

'I can't imagine what Rut wants,' Helgi said, and sighed heavily. 'She called me on Saturday evening too, remember? That time she'd forgotten – *forgotten*' – he smiled cynically – 'to tell me that Elín had disappeared a couple of times before. I suspect she still hasn't told me the whole sordid story. But perhaps things will be a bit clearer after this visit.'

'Do you think she could have done something to Elín? And that she wants to confess?'

'Impossible to tell. But I can't imagine a publisher wanting to . . . well, murder her most popular author. That just doesn't make sense.'

'What I don't understand is why the press aren't all over the investigation. It's front-page stuff, after all.'

'They will be very soon,' Helgi said, then asked: 'By the way, what are we going to do at Christmas? Have you had a chance to think it over yet?'

'Are you sure we'll still be together at Christmas?' Aníta fired back, grinning at him.

'Oh, I think there's a chance, yes. Would you like to go to Akureyri?'

'I get the impression you want to.'

'Yes, it's lovely up there. Proper snow and a great atmosphere.'

'Christmas with your mother, eh?' Aníta laughed. 'OK, let me think about it.'

'There's no rush.'

Rut sat on the sofa in the living room, still in her soaking-wet coat. She was clutching a plastic bag and looking rather embarrassed.

Aníta had made herself scarce, saying she was going to read in the bedroom, but Helgi suspected she was listening at the door. Not that he could blame her.

His gaze travelled from the plastic bag to his visitor.

Maybe he ought to invite her to take off her coat, but he was keen to get rid of her as soon as possible and didn't want to give her any excuse to linger.

'Well,' he said, glancing automatically at the clock. It was getting on for 11 p.m.

'I'm sorry to come round so late, but it's urgent, and . . . er, there's something I need to tell you.'

Could Aníta have been right? Was the woman about to confess to some dreadful crime?

And what on earth was in that bag?

Helgi felt his heart miss a beat. He might have invited a murderer into his home.

'Helgi . . . There's something about Elín . . .'

'Yes?'

Rut held out the dripping bag to him.

'Have a look at this.'

After a brief hesitation, he took it from her and peered inside the bag.

It contained what appeared to be the manuscript of a book.

He could hardly believe his eyes.

Could Elín have written a sequel to her famous series?

He put the bag down, anxious not to handle this piece of evidence more than necessary.

'Is this a new book?' he asked.

Rut nodded.

'By Elín?'

Instead of confirming, she asked:

'Helgi, does the name Marteinn Einarsson mean any-thing to you?'

2005

[hissing]

Is everything OK? Shall we carry on?
Yes.

I've really enjoyed our chat.
Yes, amazingly, it hasn't turned out to be
as much of a strain as I thought it would.
And, thank God, I'll never have to read it.

[pause]

Kristín, earlier you asked me about the
future, about my plans . . .

Did I?
I thought you did, but maybe that's a
misunderstanding on my part . . .

[pause]

Then, Elín, could you tell me something about your future plans?
You may be surprised to hear that I'm actually very busy. Idleness has always bored me. Age is an abstract concept, and you never know how long you've got left.

Are there any exciting new projects in the pipeline, then? Outside the literary realm?
Inside the literary realm, actually. I love books and always have done. I can't imagine occupying myself with anything else.

Yes, I can understand that. It's always been obvious that you have a genuine interest in writing as a form of artistic expression.
[pause]

Would you tell us about your next project, Elín? Something connected to literature, you say, but not writing?
As a matter of fact, it is writing.

What?
Yes.

Are you writing something?
A new book, yes.

[pause]

That's quite some news.
You could say that. But to me nothing is
more natural than writing. I've never
stopped. I just haven't wanted to discuss
the fact until now. Everything has its time.

**What kind of story . . . I mean, what are
you writing?**
I'm writing a crime novel.

**A new crime novel, that's amazing.
That'll be eleven altogether. When can we
expect it?**
More than eleven.

**More than eleven? But your series, that
was only ten books.**
Yes, I've written quite a bit since then,
and before that too.

Is it something we'll get to see in print?
Yes, all the books have already been
published.

**I'm sorry, now you've lost me . . . Are
these books by you – that have been
published?**
Yes, under a different name.

[pause]

You're not talking about Marteinn Einarsson, are you?
Yes, those are my books.

Good grief. I thought it was the best-kept secret in publishing.
It is. Not many people know. Now you're part of that select group. And one day your readers will be too. I'm pleased with the books, and I'm not ashamed to say so.

I believe you. But why the pseudonym, Elín?
I was happy with the original series, ten books in twenty years. No reason to complicate matters. This was a different sort of venture, initially undertaken for fun, because, take it from me, you should only write books as long as it gives you pleasure.

Did it never occur to you to reveal your secret?
No, not until now.

Why now?
It's time. You see, the thing is, Kristín,
all secrets have a way of coming out in
the end.

2012

Monday, 5 November

'Yes, I've heard of Marteinn. His books, that is,' Helgi said, beginning to have his suspicions. 'What's his connection to Elín?'

Rut didn't immediately answer. She looked almost sheepish.

'Marteinn's books, they're by Elín, you see.'

This theory had of course been aired at times over the years, along with various others – for example that a former prime minister had written them – but Helgi was completely unprepared to hear it confirmed as the truth. Sometimes, he reflected, the obvious solution was quite simply the right one.

'Elín S. Jónsdóttir and Marteinn Einarsson,' he said slowly. 'I see.'

Then he added, trying not to betray how annoyed he was: 'And it didn't occur to you to tell me this before?'

'I just couldn't. It's such a big secret. Those in the

know can be literally counted on the fingers of one hand. Me and my husband, of course, and Lovísa. And Elín's lawyer, Baldur. He helped her with some of her contracts with foreign publishers. I couldn't see how these books could have anything to do with Elín's disappearance, so I wanted to put off telling anyone for as long as possible. The more people who know, the more likely the secret is to get out.'

'I see,' Helgi said, though he didn't have much sympathy with this view. He would have preferred to have been put in the picture on day one. Rut should have trusted him with the information. 'Then why are you telling me now?' he asked. 'Why have you been sitting on this manuscript?'

'What? No, I haven't been sitting on it. Sorry, I haven't explained properly . . . The thing is, I've only just received it.'

'What?'

'Yes, it was left outside my office this morning. In a bag.'

'And it's a new book by . . . Marteinn?'

Rut nodded.

'Now you've really astonished me,' Helgi said.

'Yes, that's understandable.'

'Were you expecting this book?'

'To be honest, yes, but not necessarily straight away. We had discussed publishing a new book next year, but no one else knew that, not even my husband. Elín said she was writing it and that she was making good progress. I think we last talked about it in the summer. Anyway, she's clearly finished the book.'

'Are you sure about that?'

'Yes, I skimmed through the manuscript before ringing you. I needed to work out what it all meant. The story is complete, as far as I can tell.'

'You'll have to leave the bag with me, Rut. I hope you understand that.'

'Yes,' she said resignedly. 'Although it's the only copy, of course. The whole thing handwritten, as usual. Could I make a copy of it?'

'Allow me to take care of that,' Helgi replied firmly. He was exasperated with Rut for withholding such an important piece of evidence. And now he wanted more than anything to read the manuscript. Was it possible that there was something in it that could shed light on Elín's whereabouts?

Which brought him face to face with another, much bigger question: was there any need to investigate this disappearance?

Had Elín in fact been holed up somewhere in the countryside all this time, calmly finishing her manuscript while her friends were frantically looking for her?

'Do you think she delivered the manuscript herself?' he asked.

Again, Rut was slow to answer.

'I haven't been able to think about anything else,' she said at last. 'I suppose she must have done, but I simply can't imagine it. Usually, when she's ready to deliver, we meet up for a sort of formal handover ceremony and she entrusts me with the only copy of her new book. Then we talk about the plot, the publishing schedule, and so on. She's never left a book behind without any explanation before. Let alone practically left it in the street. No, Helgi, it's impossible to understand. Unless she wants to be lost – I have considered that possibility. That this is her way of telling us that she's all right and we can stop looking for her.'

'Do you think we should stop, Rut?'

'Honestly, I don't know. She's my friend, my best friend, and I'm worried about her. I can hardly sleep at night. And I know my husband and Lovísa feel the same. We have to find her, but . . .' After a long pause, she went on: 'The problem is, Helgi, that if Elín doesn't want us to find her, then we don't have a hope. Because she's extremely clever, you know. And I suppose there could be an explanation for all this, something that's none of our business.'

'I don't think we can call off the search just yet. Let me read the manuscript and try to figure out if it contains the missing piece of the puzzle.'

'What? Oh no, I doubt you'll find anything. I expect it's just a typical Marteinn Einarsson story. There won't be any clues hidden there, any more than in Marteinn's – I mean Elín's – other books. They're generally a great read, written with tremendous verve. Elín just can't stop writing, you see. She loves it. And you can imagine how happy I am to keep publishing her, even if readers aren't aware of it.'

'How have the books performed?'

'Pretty well. They may not reach the top of the bestseller lists like the series Elín published under her own name, but then she's never written to be popular or make money. Goodness, no. The Marteinn books haven't been as successful abroad, though they sell quite well in Britain. Perhaps they don't appeal as much to foreign readers. Who knows?'

'Are you going to publish it?'

'This book? Yes, of course. Assuming I get the manuscript back. Elín clearly wants it to come out.'

Helgi didn't comment on this assertion.

'Her last book, perhaps?'

'For God's sake, don't talk like that. I really hope not.'

'If . . . when the book is published, Rut, are you planning to reveal the secret if it turns out that Elín is dead?'

'I can't even think about that possibility,' Rut said, her voice trembling. Then she collected herself and continued more steadily: 'But the answer's no, I'm pretty sure I won't. The secret was never supposed to get out. Come to think of it, we did discuss something related to that . . .'

'Oh?'

'If she went before me, as she put it, she suggested that I simply continue publishing the Marteinn books. Let other authors have a go at writing about the main characters, using the same pen name.'

'I feel I have to ask again: was Elín ill?'

'No, to the best of my knowledge she's extremely fit for her age. She's simply the type who talks candidly about her own death. She's always been like that. Perhaps that's why she could write about death — write about it with so much insight, I mean. Helgi, can I ask you to keep this to yourself, this business of the book and Marteinn's identity?'

'We'll have to see. I'm happy for the literary world to keep its secrets, where possible. But first I need to submit the book for analysis, to find out if there's any evidence. Then I want to read it. Shall we evaluate the situation after that?'

'Still, it looks more likely now, doesn't it, that she's all right?' There was a light in Rut's eyes, he thought, a faint gleam of hope. Yet in spite of that he had to keep an open mind about the possibility that she wasn't telling him the whole truth. After all, she had twice withheld important information from him, not by lying exactly, but by failing to tell him the whole story.

Was it conceivable that she had been responsible for the death of her friend and that this whole situation was a play put on for his benefit?

He studied her, not speaking, trying to work out whether the person sitting in front of him was a murderer or just a concerned publisher and friend.

Unable to come to a conclusion, he rose to his feet.

'Let's leave it there for now, Rut. We'll talk again tomorrow.'

1977

Hulda was exhausted when she finally got there.

The fishing lodge – her destination – was a smart, modern building where she was due to stay for the next few days. Her assignment was straightforward enough, though not necessarily straightforward in practice: to guard the Prince of Wales, who was visiting for the salmon fishing.

Hulda hadn't actively chosen this assignment, but neither had she declined it when she was asked to assist. The atmosphere at work was tense these days in relation to her future in the service and, in the circumstances, she couldn't afford to refuse any jobs. A new national Criminal Investigation Department had been set up to take over all the relevant cases, but Hulda still hadn't been transferred there. No real reasons had been put forward to explain this state of affairs, but she knew that the answer was simple: she had a lot of enemies in the police, male colleagues who didn't believe a woman should be given a major role in investigations. It was, and would remain, a

231

boys' club. But she had no intention of being passed over like this and was fighting tooth and nail for her position, without going so far as to disobey orders or do anything that could justify her dismissal. Fortunately, though, she also had friends within the police; she wasn't alone in her battle, and she remained convinced that sooner or later she would get that position in CID.

Given this background, she hadn't made any objections when she heard that she was to be deployed to the east of Iceland for several days. Little Dimma had stayed behind at home with Jón, of course. She was three years old and Hulda had never been away from her for so long before. It would be a wrench, and the idea filled her with misgiving. Of course, she didn't doubt for a minute that Jón was up to the job of looking after her, but for some reason she found it terribly hard to let Dimma out of her sight. The little girl had no idea her mother was going away as Hulda cuddled her with tears in her eyes before asking Jón to take good care of her. There was a phone at the fishing lodge, according to the information she had been given, and whenever she got the chance she promised she would ring home.

Their married life mostly continued as usual, though she and Jón had been arguing more often recently about Hulda's choice of profession. Jón was insisting that her superiors' decision to block Hulda's promotion should give her pause to think carefully about her situation. Did she really want to spend her entire working life in an environment where she would never be fully accepted? Not to mention the low salary and challenging hours.

Jón's business was doing well and, in his opinion, his wife shouldn't have to go out to work while Dimma was still so young. It would make more sense for Hulda to put off looking for a job until later, then find something where her talents would be properly appreciated, as he put it. This friction at home was having a bad effect on Hulda. Perhaps a few days' break from Jón would do her good — and him too. Dimma would thrive in her father's company, although of course Hulda would miss her unbearably.

When she entered the fishing lodge where the prince was to stay, she was met by a tall, middle-aged man.

'Hulda? Are you Hulda?' he asked. It was hardly a bold guess on his part, as she was the only policewoman there.

'Yes,' she replied.

'There was a phone call for you earlier.'

She was instantly sure that Jón must have called and knew he would only have done so if something had happened. Her heart lurched painfully in her chest and she took a few more steps into the room, then drew a deep breath and tried to control the quiver in her voice as she asked: 'Who was it?'

'Some woman from Reykjavík. Elísabet, her name was. She left a phone number.'

Hulda didn't immediately recognize the name. It must be connected to work.

'Could I borrow the phone?' she asked.

'Be my guest.'

'I'm sorry to bother you, Hulda. Only, your colleagues said I could reach you at this number. Actually, they said

ragnar

you were on another job now, but I implied that it was quite urgent, although, well . . .'

The connection was poor and Hulda couldn't place the voice.

'I'm sorry, but who is this, please?'

'Elísabet Karlsdóttir. We met last summer. I was married to Hinrik, who died . . .'

This told Hulda everything she needed to know. She pictured the woman sitting in her lonely little kitchen on Kaplaskjólsvegur. Hulda's inquiries hadn't delivered any results and she had later heard that Einar Másson had been released on parole. Presumably he was walking free now. Could he have knocked on the widow's door? Told her something, even . . .

For a second Hulda thought she might have found the key that would guarantee her a place in CID. If she could solve a major case like this, surely no one could stand in her way?

'Oh, yes, right. Nice to hear from you, Elísabet. Sorry, but the connection is absolutely terrible. I'm in the east, deep in the countryside,' she said, without elaborating. 'I understand Einar has been released. Has he tried to contact you?'

'That's exactly why I'm ringing. Although I know there's nothing you can do, nothing anyone can do, I just needed to talk to somebody. I hope you can understand that.'

'Of course.' Hulda felt for the woman, whose loneliness was almost palpable over the crackling phone line. Again, Elísabet's plight made Hulda frighteningly aware of the fragility of life. It reminded her that she must do everything in her power to look after Jón and Dimma and hold them close. She couldn't be alone like this poor woman, couldn't even contemplate such a tragic fate.

'He's dead.'

'Hinrik?'

'Einar. Einar's dead.'

Hulda wasn't sure she'd heard right.

'Is Einar Másson dead?' she asked, inadvertently raising her voice. 'Hadn't he recently got out of prison?'

'Yes, but he only lasted two weeks. I hear he drank himself to death. I just wanted to know if he maybe told you something before . . .'

'I'm sorry, Elísabet. He had nothing to say.' *And he won't say anything now . . .*

'Oh, well, I was afraid of that. Then it's all over, Hulda. I'll never get justice now. Sorry, of course it's not your fault – of course it's not your fault. I won't disturb you any longer.'

'You're not disturbing me. I'm so sorry about this, Elísabet. I wish I could help you.'

'Thanks for returning my call, Hulda.'

TUESDAY

2012

Tuesday, 6 November

Helgi was woken by the rain; it was still tipping it down out there. The curtains were open in the bedroom and the rain rattled on the glass, streaming down into the dark winter morning. At this time of year, it was always a long wait for daylight.

He turned over, intending to wake Aníta, only to discover that she had gone.

She did this from time to time when she stayed over, slipping away without a word, generally because she needed to go home to get ready for work. Yesterday evening they had finally had a proper conversation about her moving in with him, and planned for it to happen before Christmas, if possible.

Now that they had made the decision, Helgi couldn't wait to have Aníta living with him in the little flat. Her presence made him so ridiculously happy. Even a dismal rainy day like today couldn't rob him of the feeling. He eased himself out of bed, still groggy with sleep, but already looking forward to this evening. He just had to be patient. Maybe he should start the day by going for a run in the rain; brave the weather rather than cowering under the covers.

Getting back to the warm flat after his run, drenched with rain and sweat, had felt so good, with the endorphins pumping through his body and the prospect of a hot shower to look forward to. It was a different story later that morning, when Helgi dashed the short distance from his car to the police station. Despite sprinting, he was wet through by the time he reached the entrance.

His coat and trousers were sodden, and so was his shirt where his coat hadn't protected him. The atmosphere among his colleagues seemed rather subdued too, he thought, as if the heavy clouds had dragged everyone down with them. He had brought Elín's – or Marteinn's – manuscript with him, still in its plastic bag, and was intending to ask Forensics to examine it for potential evidence before he got down to reading it.

'There's a woman waiting to see you, Helgi,' one of his colleagues said.

'Sorry?'

'She's in the interview room.'

'What's her name?'

'Can't remember.'

Helgi dropped by his office and hung up his coat. There would be a puddle on the floor by the end of the day. He put down his bag too and took out a whodunnit,

Brat Farrar by Josephine Tey. To his relief, it hadn't got wet. It was yet another story that centred on a missing-persons case. A young boy vanishes and many years later a stranger turns up, claiming to be him in order to get his hands on the family fortune.

He was fully expecting to find Rut waiting for him. Perhaps she had remembered something else that she had 'forgotten' to tell him.

Alternatively, she could have come in to confess belatedly to a crime.

The police were planning to issue a press release about Elín's disappearance later in the week in order to appeal to the public for information. Someone had to have seen or heard something. Helgi was dreading the media frenzy: he would be under siege from reporters.

But, with any luck, Rut was about to change the course of the investigation.

He opened the door to the interview room, where, to his astonishment, he saw not Rut but Kristín Unnur from the radio.

She was sitting at the table, looking rather downcast, but raised her eyes for a moment when Helgi entered.

'Hi,' she said in a low voice.

'Kristín, I wasn't expecting you.' Helgi took a seat opposite her.

'No, I wasn't expecting to be here today either.'

It was clear from her appearance that she had been caught in the rain as well, her hair and coat dripping. 'What can I do for you?' Helgi asked. He had never seriously entertained the suspicion that Kristín might be directly involved in the case, despite the fact that she had the most to gain from it. By far the most, in fact. The previous day he had finally received all the information from Elín's bank – after chasing them several times – and discovered that her accounts contained around two million euros, presumably from international royalties, in addition to which she owned her house outright. If Elín did turn out to be dead, Kristín would stand to inherit a substantial fortune.

She didn't immediately respond to Helgi's question.

The only thing breaking the silence in the hot, muggy room was the roar of the wind and rain outside. Helgi got up and pulled back the curtains to admit some light. He remained there for a moment or two, staring out at the drab, grey view. The miserable weather, the traffic lights, the cars, the blocks of concrete – there was nothing out there to gladden the eye. He felt an overpowering longing to go home and crawl back into bed with his book.

'There's something we need to discuss,' Kristín said at last, her voice sounding stronger than before.

Helgi put aside his speculation that she might be responsible somehow for Elín's disappearance. It seemed too far-fetched.

Kristín was silent again for a moment, then took a deep breath.

'I met Elín once, as I told you.'

'Right. Through work.'

She nodded.

'A radio interview?'

'No, actually. This was in 2005, before I started working for the radio. After Elín had given up writing.'

'Seven years ago, in other words?'

'Yes. I'd been working as a journalist for several years, for various different papers, though mostly at *DV*. Then one day Elín rang me out of the blue, saying she'd read one of my feature interviews and had been very taken with my style and approach, or something like that. Anyway, she flattered me, and no writer minds receiving praise from a renowned stylist like Elín S. Jónsdóttir, I can tell you.' There was a brief hint of a smile.

'I believe you,' Helgi remarked.

'She said she didn't give many interviews, in fact she'd given up the bad habit, as she put it, after her last book had come out. But she would be prepared to talk to me at some point if it would suit me. I also remember her asking whether I had any say over where and when an interview would appear. At first, I thought maybe she didn't want it to be in *DV*, but in some glossy magazine perhaps. But that wasn't the reason at all, as it later transpired.'

When he entered the room, Helgi hadn't for a minute expected to hear a story like this from Kristín. Plainly, she was planning to spin it out and keep him in suspense for as long as possible, just like Elín manipulating the readers of her novels.

'I assume you accepted her request,' he prompted.

'Yes, you bet I did. I wasn't going to miss out on an opportunity like that. I had visions of trying to sell the interview to the highest bidder, though I was still employed by *DV* at the time. At any rate, I didn't intend to tell my editors about it immediately but to play it by ear. Besides, I didn't know when Elín would make herself available for our chat or whether she was even serious.'

'And was she serious?'

'Yes. She wanted to arrange a time straight away. We met up two weeks later. I suspected she wanted to give me a chance to read her books because I hadn't read all of them. And I made good use of those two weeks, managing to get through the entire series as well as some old interviews with her. You could say I became an instant expert on Elín S. Jónsdóttir. Then we had our meeting.'

Kristín broke off to take a sip of the coffee that some-one had clearly offered her while she was waiting.

'Our conversation took place at her house. Have you been there?'

'Yes. It's a beautiful place.'

'It certainly is. A real writer's house was the impression I got.'

'Which, it seems, could one day be yours.'

Helgi instantly regretted his remark. Kristín stopped short, as if it simply hadn't occurred to her that the house would be hers along with most of the other assets – if Elín did turn out to be dead.

'We sat in her study.' Kristín's voice had acquired a dif-ferent rhythm now. 'I remember it so well. The walls were lined with books and the computer wasn't even on her desk. She handwrote all her novels, you know.'

Helgi nodded.

'We spent a long time together. I took along a cassette

recorder that I used to use for interviews, all very old school. Elín set a condition at the beginning that we weren't to discuss her private life. Of course, that was a bit disappointing, but it wasn't a deal-breaker. I found it fascinating enough just to be allowed to sit with her and take an exclusive interview. It started well, though I can remember being rather nervous; I felt like I was taking an exam and had to be at the top of my game. Elín was very nice and reacted well to all my questions – except when I accidentally strayed into areas that she considered too personal. Apart from that, she was very open from the outset, and I had begun to visualize making a splash with a brilliant feature interview. It tickled my vanity, as I'm sure you'll understand. I'd never had a proper exclusive as a journalist, but I was hoping this would be my big break.'

'I see,' Helgi said, taking care to put his next question tactfully, as he didn't want to offend the woman. 'I have to admit that the interview passed me by at the time. And I haven't come across it, though of course I haven't tried to track down all the old interviews with Elín in researching the background to this case. I expect it was well received, though, wasn't it?' He smiled at Kristín.

She shook her head. 'No, the interview has never been published.'

'What?'

'Not yet, anyway.'

'Hang on, I don't quite follow. You took the interview, but she banned you from publishing it? Or you didn't want to . . .'

'She didn't exactly ban me. She just set a further condition.'

Helgi leaned forwards over the table. This felt almost like being in one of Elín's novels, in a plot she had spun.

'What condition?' he asked eagerly.

'The interview wasn't to appear until after her death.'

'OK.'

'That's why I asked if the police believed she was dead when we met . . . because of the interview, not the inheritance. It took me a while to assimilate what had happened. And I had to do a lot of thinking before coming here today. I didn't want to break trust. You have to tread carefully when it comes to sources, even in a case like this which doesn't involve anonymity so much as a rather unusual condition. I wasn't at all sure I ought to discuss it with you, but in the end I felt it was the right thing to do. I could hardly sleep last night I've been so worried. The interview has been preying on my mind ever since you told me yesterday that Elín had gone missing.'

'Thank you for coming in, Kristín. I appreciate it. Finding Elín is our priority, but, to be blunt, I'm afraid she may be dead.'

The uncharitable thought occurred to Helgi that choosing this moment to break confidentiality would suit Kristín very well if, as a result, the police could confirm that Elín was dead.

First, though, he wanted to know if there had been anything potentially enlightening in the interview, assuming she was going to let him read it.

'When she talked to you, did she reveal anything

startling or of particular interest? I mean, can you understand what would have prompted her to make such an
odd request?'

As he spoke, he became aware of the rain again. Far
from letting up, it sounded as if it was intensifying.

'Yes. She was very frank about a number of things.
For example, she told me she was writing another series,
under the pseudonym Marteinn Einarsson.'

'Ah, yes.'

'You don't seem surprised. I thought it was a well-kept
secret?'

'I suppose that's now' – Helgi paused to count – 'a total
of maybe seven people who are in the know.'

'I haven't said a word to anyone, but I've always bought
the books when they came out. Great stories, though
quite different from the old series.'

'Of course, that could be the explanation . . .'

'Of what?' Kristín asked.

'The reason why she didn't want the interview to be
published in her lifetime.'

'Well, possibly, but I don't think so. Because that wasn't
the biggest secret.'

'Oh?'

'Yes. You see, she dropped a complete bombshell at
the end. I'm sure that's why she wanted to delay publication. Some secrets are too explosive to reveal.'

'Can you tell me in spite of that? At least give me a
brief account of what she said. Or let me read the interview for myself?'

'I haven't transcribed it; I never got round to that.

There didn't seem to be any point, since Elín was still going strong.' Kristín sighed. 'I have to admit that it's been weighing on my mind. I'm not sure Elín fully appreciated how hard it is to carry around a timebomb like that year after year, my thoughts constantly coming back to her. I've taken great care of the recording. When she originally offered me the interview, I thought maybe she was ill, even dying, but clearly that wasn't the case. She just rang me out of the blue, then proceeded to tell me her life story, pretty much. She was an unusual person. But she made an impression on me and I found myself sympathizing with her. A great subject for a feature interview, that's what I remember thinking at the time. And I've often thought about her since then but never got round to picking up the phone.'

'It's often the way.'

'I regret it now, though – God, how I regret it. If she is dead . . .'

'Don't feel too bad, Kristín. I very much doubt she was waiting for a phone call from you. You kept her secret for her and—'

Kristín shook her head and, to his surprise, Helgi noticed a tear trickling down her cheek.

When she didn't say anything, he seized the chance to ask: 'Can I listen to the recording?'

Kristín nodded.

'Yes, I was intending to let you hear it.'

'Thanks,' he said, and waited. He mustn't give her the idea that he was putting pressure on her. It seemed the recording might hold some answers, but Kristín was clearly distressed by the situation and he didn't want to risk frightening her off.

'I listened to it myself yesterday evening, after you came to see me at the studio,' she said at last. 'I hadn't heard it for years, though the conversation had stayed with me. I felt as though I remembered some of what she'd said word for word, but maybe it wasn't always like that. I've got it here in my bag. The cassette player and the tape.'

'OK.'

'But there was something else I wanted to talk to you about first, if that's all right?'

'Sure.'

'As you can imagine, I've been going over and over this in my head, Helgi. You talked about a lot of money, and even her house too. It's completely over the top, such a mad thing for her to have done.'

'Yes.'

'Anyway, as I said, I went back and listened to the tape. Then I read up on Elín again. Found some old interviews. There were no real clues there. You see, I'd spotted – or at least I believed I'd spotted – certain clues in my conversation with Elín. And I had to follow them up . . .'

She was silent for a long moment. Helgi didn't say a word, just tuned in to the drumming of the rain.

Finally, Kristín continued: 'I needed a little time to pluck up my courage.' She laughed and wiped the tear from her cheek. 'There I was, an adult, too afraid to confront the truth. Ridiculous.'

Helgi gave her an encouraging smile.

'That's nothing to be ashamed of. It must require quite an adjustment, learning about an inheritance like that, the whole thing so—'

She interrupted him, as if she wasn't even listening: '*You never asked.*'

Helgi opened his mouth to say something, but Kristín went on:

'*You never asked.* That's what my parents said to me when I went to see them early this morning. And they also said they'd promised never to tell. The whole thing was meant to be kept quiet. *But it's not as important now, and we can't stay silent for ever*, my dad said to me. Or something like that. I don't remember the exact words, but then I don't think I've ever experienced anything as shattering as this morning's revelations.'

'You don't mean . . .'

Kristín nodded.

'Yes. They say I'm adopted.' Another tear began to slide down her cheek. 'Mum and Dad. Now they tell me. I don't think they ever would have let on if I hadn't asked.'

'So you believe Elín's your mother?'

'I know for a fact she is. They told me. They've known all these years.'

'That must have been quite a shock,' Helgi said, and then it dawned on him why Kristín had appeared so familiar the first time he saw her. She reminded him, quite simply, of Elín.

'You can say that all right. And I don't know if I'll ever get a chance to meet her again . . . . All I have is that interview, nothing else . . . I don't understand why she didn't say anything, why she didn't get in touch. Though apparently she'd promised my parents never to tell me – that was the condition they made. They wanted to decide for themselves when and if they should break it to me. Like I say, I don't think it would ever have happened if I hadn't demanded an answer.'

'Well, with any luck, Elín's OK. I'm confident that you'll still have a chance to see her again,' Helgi said, against his better instincts.

Kristín shrugged.

'Did they say anything about . . . your father?' he asked, conscious of how delicate a subject this was.

'Could we open a window?' Kristín asked abruptly.

'Sure.' Helgi rose to his feet and let in some fresh air. The soothingly monotonous sound of the rain carried into the room, bringing with it a strange sense of peace.

'They don't know,' Kristín said after a moment. 'Haven't a clue. Elín didn't tell them, and I doubt I'll ever find out now. Except maybe through a DNA test, I suppose. But I don't even know where to start looking.' She leaned forward, burying her face in her hands. 'I just feel completely lost. Like Elín.'

'Should we maybe listen to the recording now?' Helgi asked. His thoughts were racing. He would have a lot of decisions to make after this conversation was over. Like whether to reveal Elín's secret to her friends. Unless they were already aware of the existence of a child? And who the hell was Kristín's father? Two men immediately sprang to mind: Thor and Baldur the lawyer. The list of possibilities might be much longer, though. Chances were it was someone Helgi had never heard of.

'She went to Ísafjördur,' Kristín said, as if she hadn't heard his question. 'She referred to the fact in our interview. She was there for just over a year, teaching at the school. So I must have been born there: the timing appears to be right.'

Rut had told Helgi about Elín's sojourn in the West Fjords, about her disappearing act. She had gone to Ísafjördur – to have a baby, as Helgi now knew. After all, she had been unmarried and times had been different then, but, even so, Helgi found it hard to understand why she had decided to go into hiding and conceal her pregnancy like that. Certainly, none of her friends had said a word to him about Elín being pregnant while at university. Perhaps she hadn't let on to a soul.

One riddle had been solved, but this had only resulted in another.

It seemed that Elín's life was like that: one big conundrum.

'I've never been there,' Kristín said. 'To Ísafjördur. Elín asked me if I had, all the time aware that I'd been born and spent my first weeks of life there. It was clever of her to invite me to take that interview with her. It's so obvious that she wanted to get to know me, don't you think?'

'Yes,' Helgi said consolingly. 'Quite obvious. She gets to meet you and tell you her life story, then puts you in her will. I'm guessing she must have thought about you a lot. And still does. Hopefully.'

Kristín smiled.

'Shall we listen to it?'

She reached for her bag and took out a battered cassette player.

'Luckily, it still works. But I need to make a copy, to be on the safe side.'

'We can do that for you,' Helgi said gently. He had no intention of letting her take the recording off the premises, especially if there was something on it that could shed light on Elín's whereabouts.

'Yes, maybe. Obviously, I need to have a copy of the interview.' After a moment, she added: 'And if she's dead, I'll have to publish it, as she asked. I can't let her down.'

Helgi hadn't thought that far. No doubt he could withhold the recording if necessary, in spite of any objections Kristín might make, but he could hardly prevent the interview from appearing in the press, sooner or later. But maybe that wouldn't hurt.

'Here it is.'

She pressed a button and turned up the volume. The hissing of the tape was in perfect harmony with the noise of the rain outside.

2005

[hissing]

**Hang on, I'm not sure it's working. OK,
I think it is. Thanks for getting in
touch, Elín. I often find it best to dive
straight in at the deep end. The first
question I've got written here is as
follows: why crime novels?**
Why, indeed.

[pause]

**Let me just check it's definitely
recording.**

[hissing]

2012

Tuesday, 6 November

Helgi was transported back to the days at his parents' house in Akureyri, when he used to sit beside an open window, the rain falling outside, listening to a detective serial on the radio. Only now he was listening to the voice of the missing author.

There was an air of mystery over the whole affair; riddles on every side.

As a child, all he'd had to do was listen and everything would come right in the end; in a few short weeks the solution would be revealed.

This time, though, it was up to him to solve the mystery.

2005

[hissing]

I'm happiest in that vague borderland
between daylight and shadows; that's
where I go in search of stories to tell,
particularly stories about crimes. I
used to read all kinds of books before I
began writing myself, and what I noticed
was that the ones that really held my
attention, that made the most indelible
impression on me, were the ones that were
concerned with justice and punishment.
That's the theme of most novels, one way
or another; crime is the driving force of
the narrative . . .

2012

Tuesday, 6 November

Kristín turned over the tape.

Helgi couldn't tell how long they'd been sitting there listening, as he had been transported to another world. For a while, he'd had to struggle against drowsiness despite the atmosphere of suspense and was grateful for the open window admitting a little fresh air.

'This is the last part,' Kristín said. 'It'll be quite an interview when I finally get it down on paper . . .' Although she spoke flippantly, there was a hint of sadness in her voice.

Elín had talked about her writing, her career, her studies and teaching, her pseudonym – everything apart from her private life. Helgi was still none the wiser about that side, as she kept it hidden in the shadows she had mentioned.

She still hadn't revealed any startling secrets, apart from the one about Marteinn Einarsson's identity.

There was nothing that could explain her disappearance, nothing to suggest she could have been murdered . . .

2005

[hissing]

I think I've about run out of questions, Elín. I've kept you far too long, but it's been so enjoyable, and fascinating to hear about the extraordinary life you've led.
Extraordinary . . . yes, sometimes, I suppose. But isn't it the same for everyone – that we all have extraordinary experiences at one time or another? It may be a cliché, but life is always a mixture of sunshine and showers.

I'll let you read the interview when I've written it up. There's no rush, I assume? I can't quite see where it would be best placed. It won't necessarily . . .
We can talk about that at the end. You'll recall that I mentioned two conditions

when we first spoke? I haven't brought up
the second one yet.

**Oh, yes, OK. I remember. That . . .
that's fine.**
First, I wanted to tell you a story,
Kristín, if you have time.

**Yes, of course. Shall I turn off the
recording?**
No, please don't. This will all belong in
the interview, when the time comes. I have
a crime story for you, to finish off with.
It's a story that's never found its way
into any of my books and never will. But
you'll get to tell it.

I'm intrigued . . .
The story begins in 1965 with a group
of friends, three law students,
one of whom has a brilliant idea.
The brilliant . . . well, that's
debatable . . . idea of how to commit the
perfect crime. I don't really know why.
Perhaps it was just for the thrill
of it – that's my suspicion. As a way of
spicing up their life, or simply because
it was possible. Sometimes people do
things just because they can. Do you know
what I mean?

Yes, I suppose so.
Well, anyway, the law students discuss the
idea, initially as a joke, I believe, but
gradually it becomes apparent that they're
serious. There's money at stake too, and
of course that can be a big motivating
factor. Eventually it turns out that there
is an actual plan to commit a serious
crime, but a victimless crime, as it was
described in my hearing.

Hang on, what was the crime?
To rob a bank. A local branch on a quiet
street, not much security in evidence –
an easy target, in other words. Lots of
businesses deposited their money there –
that was the justification I heard. That
it would be a piece of cake; the perfect
crime, in other words. Although I got wind
of it, I had no intention of taking part.
All I was interested in at the time was
finishing my degree. I was still aiming to
become a lawyer. But they were my friends,
so I watched from the sidelines; saw it
become a reality, little by little, saw
the idea taking shape. But I didn't say a
word, didn't lift a finger, perhaps because
I thought it was all a big joke. Though
perhaps on some level I knew better. But
then, how well do we know our friends when

it comes down to it? And when do we stop
standing by them? When do we stop trying
to step in and save them from danger?

**This sounds like good material for a
novel . . .**
Then one morning it happened. A bank
robbery in broad daylight. The country was
in shock.

**Wait a minute, I'm not sure I've ever
heard about that.**
Maybe not, no. After all, this was before
you were born, but people had never
experienced anything like it, not in quiet
little Iceland.

**There must surely have been bank robberies
in the past?**
Not many armed robberies, not in those
days. And that wasn't all: one of the bank
staff died.

Oh, I see. That's terrible.
Things went dreadfully wrong. A victimless
crime, they'd said. But a brave cashier –
maybe he was a security guard too – tried
to resist them and a shot was fired.

Wait, you knew about this . . .?

Yes, I knew about it, not precisely when
it was supposed to happen, but I knew
about the preparations and of course I
knew the names of the bank robbers. The
name of the killer. But I didn't say
anything. Remember what I said just now:
when do we stop standing by our friends?
What do you say to that, Kristín?

Weren't they ever caught?
One of the robbers was caught, yes. But
only one. He was sentenced to prison for
murder; he got sixteen years.

What's his name?
His name was Einar. He was a good friend
of mine, a sweet boy, from a hard-up
family. Like me, he meant to become a
lawyer. He was a good student. Perhaps he
was led astray by the money . . . as if it
could ever pay to rob a bank.

Is he dead?
Yes, he died a long time ago.

**What happened? Did he serve his full
sentence?**
He served ten and a half years, or
thereabouts. Then he was released on
parole. You know, I never went to visit

him in prison. I didn't dare, didn't want
to get involved. I had long ago given up
my law studies; I couldn't continue – for
various reasons, including this. I was
afraid. I wanted to try and live my life
in peace without being implicated, even
indirectly, in a bank robbery and murder.
I just wanted to forget about it, but of
course it's been preying on my mind ever
since. I didn't do anything wrong except
keep quiet. But sometimes that's a big
enough sin on its own.

What happened to Einar?
He just wasted away in prison. He couldn't
take it. I'm told his health gradually
broke down. Yet he survived long enough to
walk free for a brief time, only to die
shortly afterwards. There was no single
reason, it was the whole situation. I
didn't have the courage to visit him even
when he got out of prison, I kept putting
it off . . .

**Didn't he ever reveal his accomplice's
identity?**
Never said a word. Friends stand by one
another, you see. He was unlucky; the
police caught him. I suppose he must have
known his life was ruined, but he didn't

want to wreck anyone else's. I think I can
understand that. He might have received a
more lenient sentence, though he'd always
have had to do a long, long stint inside.
Still, a shorter sentence might have saved
his life. Because who would be able to
cope with the prospect of being locked up
for sixteen years?

**What about you, Elín? If you don't mind my
asking . . . why did you never speak up?**
I've often wondered that. I think there
were a lot of reasons. They were my
friends, my best friends, and, to be
honest, I wasn't sure it was my job to
report them. I hadn't done anything
wrong, I'd only heard about their plans
and hadn't taken them seriously, but when
it was all over, of course I knew what
had happened. What would you have done?
Should I have rung the police and sent
my friends to prison? The poor cashier
was already dead. It was too late to save
anyone's life. But as the years wore on I
came to the realization that I couldn't
take a secret like that to my grave.
Perhaps I should have written about it in
fictionalized form, but that didn't seem
appropriate. My books are an outlet for my
imagination, my creativity and artistic

talents, whereas what had happened was all too real.

But it's all right for me to tell people about this in the interview?
Yes, when the time comes. I trust you to do justice to the story. The truth needs to come out.

Your friend, Einar, who was arrested and died. Wasn't he guilty?
Yes, certainly, he was involved. But it wasn't his idea. And I know he didn't fire the gun.

But wasn't he convicted for that?
Yes, and he never pointed the finger at anyone else. Maybe I should have intervened at that stage, but I didn't have any proof, only the testimony of my friends about what had happened. Einar committed armed robbery, but he didn't kill anyone.

Are you willing to tell me who his accomplice was? The name of the man who killed the bank employee?

[pause]

It wasn't a man, it was a woman.

[pause]

It was my best friend. Her name's
Lovísa. And we're still best friends.
I'm finding it hard to say this aloud
even now, after all these years, despite
knowing it won't appear in print straight
away . . . She's done well for herself,
in spite of everything. She passed
her law exams in style, the only one
of us three, then later went to work
for the courts and eventually rose to
become a judge. An illustrious career
by any standards. She's taught law,
too, and written academic books. She'll
never tell anyone what happened that
day in 1965. That's why it's up to me
to do it.

**You're still best friends, you say . . . Do
you ever talk about this?**
No, never. It's too difficult. Sometimes
it's best to pretend it never happened.
But I'm going to warn her next time we
meet that I've given an interview and told
the whole story. Then she'll know that
justice will come for her in the end.
But I'm also going to reassure her that
it won't come out until after I'm gone.
I know it sounds cowardly, in a way, not

wanting to be around to help her deal with
the situation, but in all honesty this was
her mistake, not mine.

**What, what do you mean? You're . . . you're
not dying, are you?**
No, fortunately. Lovísa's pretty fit too.
Maybe she'll die before me and then she'll
never have to suffer for it – not in that
sense, if you follow me.

**Then I'm afraid I don't quite understand,
Elín, why the interview won't appear until
after you've gone?**
Ah, you see, that's my second condition.
I realize it could create quite a
sensation, with you shedding light on a
cold case, a major case, that most people
have probably forgotten about these days.
But you're just going to have to wait and
keep the recording safe. I trust you to
find the right way of presenting the story
when the time comes.

**OK, I see . . . frankly, I'm a bit taken
aback.**
You needn't be so polite; I know it's
unfair and that I should have been
straight with you from the beginning. But
it has to be this way. The secret has to

be exposed one day, but I don't want to see it. I'm too fond of Lovísa.

I think we should stop now, then, don't you? Was there anything else that . . .? Yes, let's stop now. That'll do.

[hissing]

2012

Tuesday, 6 November

After his meeting with Kristín, Helgi hurried down the stairs at the police station.

He had managed to convince her that the recording was best kept with him for the time being but promised to have a copy made and sent to her at the first opportunity. He could deal with that later. For now, the priority was to hang on to this precious piece of evidence – and to go and scc Lovísa.

That warm, kindly woman – mother, grandmother, respected lawyer and judge. Helgi pictured her, thinking that it would never have crossed his mind that she had a human life on her conscience. Perhaps even two lives.

Surely this must be the explanation? The missing piece of the puzzle.

Elín knew something that no one else must find out – the truth which not only could but would ruin Lovísa's life. And now Elín had vanished.

Helgi ran back outside into the rain.

His coat had hardly had a chance to dry.

And yet, he thought, it didn't add up, not entirely.

If the recording was to be believed, Lovísa must have known that it wasn't in her interest for Elín to die, since her death would precipitate a chain of events that would result in the exposure of Lovísa's crime. It was pure co-incidence, or luck, that Kristín had decided to speak to the police now, although Elín's fate was still unknown. The interview wasn't supposed to be published until after Elín's death, so what possible motivation would Lovísa have had to kill her best friend?

Helgi drove fast, almost recklessly, once he had pulled out into the traffic. Visibility was limited in the rain and the roads were congested, but he was impelled by a sense of urgency to see Lovísa as soon as possible. The radio was on in the car, booming in the rain.

Perhaps Kristín was about to go on air at this very moment. He wondered if she would still feel like work-ing from nine to five once her bank account was full of money.

Was it a hundred per cent certain that Elín was dead?

Not for the first time, he felt as if he were immersed in one of Elín's novels. The last case, a mystery that reached beyond the grave.

He was well on his way to the suburb of Fossvogur, weaving through the traffic, when his phone rang.

'Helgi?'

'Aníta, hi. Look, I'm in a hurry. Can we talk later?'

'No, wait, have you got a minute?'

He slowed down a little, not wanting to risk an accident. The streets were wet and slippery and his car had already skidded when taking a bend.

'Yes, but only one minute. What's the matter? Is everything OK?'

'What, oh, yes, fine, of course. It's just that I went out to get a sandwich just now and I thought I saw her.'

'Who?' he asked, though of course he knew the answer.

'Bergthóra.'

'Are you sure, Aníta?'

'No, the thing is, I'm not quite sure. She was in the car park and I was going in the other direction, and the rain's so heavy it was hard to see. Maybe I'm just being silly . . .'

He simply didn't have time to deal with this now, especially if Aníta had become paranoid and started seeing Bergthóra on every street corner. Not that this was Aníta's fault. Bergthóra had given her a nasty fright with her unsettling visit – and the incident on the bus – and Aníta clearly hadn't got over it yet. Whether or not Bergthóra had been in the car park, Helgi made up his mind once and for all: this weekend he was going round to the flat to have it out with her. Make her understand that this behaviour was totally unacceptable. If necessary, he would even consider a restraining order, though that was probably a bit over the top. Besides, he'd never made a formal complaint about the violence she had used against him, or mentioned it to anyone except the psychologist he was no longer seeing.

He and Aníta had to be allowed to get on with their lives in peace, though. Perhaps they should slip away on holiday, go for a long weekend abroad. Somewhere with decent weather.

'Can we talk it over this evening, Aníta?' he asked. 'It must have been somebody else. I can't believe Berg-thóra's stalking you.'

'It's such an uncomfortable feeling, but, OK . . . And there's another thing. On Sunday evening—'

'I'll cook something nice for us, OK?' he interrupted, afraid of having an accident if he didn't concentrate on his driving. 'But I'm afraid I've got to go now.'

'Yes, please. OK, let's talk about it later.' He could almost hear her smiling at the other end.

Helgi drove into the Fossvogur neighbourhood. It was a quiet old suburb, hidden away in a valley of sorts, so the weather there was always a little kinder than elsewhere in Reykjavík, and in a town so close to the Arctic, every little helped. This was somewhere he could imagine living in future if he didn't move back to Akureyri. He hadn't quite adapted to Reykjavík. The trouble with the capital was that it just wasn't Akureyri. The weather was too dreary in summer; he missed the long sunny days up north. And, conversely, there wasn't enough snow in winter. Helgi wouldn't dream of cele-brating Christmas anywhere other than among the deep, picture-book drifts in Akureyri, where he could nip out to the little bookshop and settle down among the dusty volumes to read the treasures in his collection. There was a lot to be said for a simple life.

He drove up to Lovísa's house, this time without having called ahead to announce his arrival.

He parked nearby, though not in the drive, and rang the doorbell.

Lovísa wasn't long in appearing. She greeted him with a smile, her brow wrinkling quizzically, her eyes radiating kindness. Could this woman really be a murderer? Even if it was true, he wasn't afraid of her. In fact, he found it hard to believe she would hurt a fly.

'Hello, Helgi, should I have been expecting you? Sometimes I worry that I've started forgetting appointments; it's my age, you know. Come in, but please take off your shoes, if you wouldn't mind. It's so wet out there.'

'No problem. No, you didn't forget, I just happened to be passing. I have a few questions about Elín, if that's all right with you?'

'Of course. I'm on my way to Florida in ten days' time.' Her gaze darted to the wet, grey world outside the large sitting-room window. 'I can't wait to see the sun.'

'I've never been there myself. I'll have to remedy that.' Though he guessed that holidays of the kind Lovísa took would be considerably beyond the budget of a police officer. Lovísa had done well for herself, as Elín had said in the interview: a large family home, an unblemished record at work, a family, no hint of skeletons in her cupboard.

'No news of Elín,' she said. At first, Helgi thought it was a question, then he realized it sounded more like a statement.

'No, we haven't heard from her,' he replied. 'I'm afraid. But we're not giving up hope. Could you remind me when you last saw her?'

Lovísa seemed a little surprised by his question and didn't immediately answer.

'You went for a hike up Mount Esja,' Helgi prompted, 'then met for coffee two weeks ago, but—'

'Yes, as I told you the other day. I haven't forgotten; there's nothing wrong with my memory in that respect. We did a day trip to Esja on Saturday, 20 October, as I said, but you already have that information, Helgi. Then we met for coffee a couple of days later, which would have been, let me see, 23 October.'

'At Kaffivagninn, am I right?'

'Yes, as always.'

'Then a week later, she didn't show up.'

'That's right.' Lovísa seemed suddenly on her guard. She had been friendlier when he first arrived.

Just then, Helgi had an idea and decided to test it, even though it would require telling a lie. But he reassured himself that the end justified the means.

'As it happens, I spoke to the girl who was working at Kaffivagninn on 23 October and she doesn't remember seeing the two of you. Yet it was a quiet day and of course she would have recognized Elín, as she's so well known.'

Helgi was rather pleased with this lie. He had a hunch that he had hit on the truth. That it had gone something like this: Lovísa had murdered her friend on the mountain, then pretended they'd met for coffee as usual three days later. It wasn't until Thor drew attention to Elín's absence that Lovísa had been forced to admit that Elín hadn't turned up the following Tuesday . . .

'I'm not sure what you're getting at,' Lovísa said after a long pause. 'You're saying she didn't see us?'

'Were you really there, Lovísa? You know, I think Elín's been missing for longer than we've been told.'

Lovísa was silent.

'There's something else we need to talk about too.'

She kept her gaze fixed on him.

'I had a meeting earlier with a woman who took an interview with Elín some years ago.'

The blood drained from Lovísa's face.

It was as if she had been robbed of all her strength.

Helgi had never seen words have such an immediate effect.

'I see.' Lovísa got to her feet with some difficulty. 'Sorry, I forgot to offer you coffee, Helgi. I can be so absent-minded. Would you like a cup?'

'Black, please.' Despite the warmth in the room, he was shivering in his damp clothes.

He stayed where he was while Lovísa vanished into the kitchen, and surveyed the paintings by her late husband that graced the walls. A talented artist, no doubt about it. Perhaps a little on the modern side for a house of this sort; the canvases didn't quite go with the period furnishings.

Judging by her reaction, Lovísa must know what was coming.

'Here you are, Helgi. Good and hot. This is wretched weather we're having.'

He took a sip. The coffee was unusually strong but not at all bitter, yet even so it couldn't quite drive out the chill.

'Were you aware of this interview?' he asked, returning to sober reality.

There was a lengthy pause before Lovísa answered.

'Yes, I'd heard about it. I don't suppose there's much point in denying that now.' She looked a little dazedly at her surroundings, perhaps feeling as if her world was collapsing around her.

'Did Elín tell you about it?' Helgi prompted.

Lovísa nodded.

'I've listened to it. She talks about you.'

'Yes, I see . . .' Lovísa murmured.

'About something that happened in 1965. Does that ring a bell?'

'I don't know what to say, Helgi. It was a long time ago. Does it matter any more? I've made a living since time out of mind from judging people and sending them to prison for sins big and small, but I've never been able to judge myself. I've just had to live with my guilt. Can you understand that?'

'Yes.'

Helgi took another mouthful of coffee. Warmth was slowly but surely returning to his body.

'How did it happen, Lovísa?'

'What?'

'The robbery.'

She was silent for a long time, staring into space as if trying to decide whether she could bring herself to talk about her past sins. She must be well aware that it paid to work with the police when the game was up.

'I don't know,' she said at last. 'A bad idea. We're

immortal when we're young, Helgi. You're still quite young yourself. Then, without warning, you realize that you're not going to live for ever; that you're going to disappear one day but that your sins won't.'

'Did you shoot the man?'

Another long pause.

'I did. I don't know why Einar didn't give me away. We never discussed it. He was fond of me. I would have looked after him when he got out, but he just died, the poor boy. Maybe he never had a chance. I feel responsible for that too, you know.'

'The robbery is outside the statute of limitations now, I believe.'

'Yes, that's right,' Lovísa replied. 'But murder isn't. Not that that's what really matters. What really matters is one's reputation. I have to admit that I was hoping I'd be able to wait this out.'

'How?'

'I haven't been entirely well for the last few years and I gather that I have, at most, one good year left.'

'I'm sorry to hear that, Lovísa.'

'That's life. Remember, we're all mortal; you just haven't realized it yet. It's not a big deal.'

'Is Elín dead?'

Lovísa didn't answer.

Perhaps he should give her more time. He wasn't in any particular hurry.

'I met her daughter,' he said, to disconcert Lovísa a little.

'What?'

'Elín's daughter.'

Lovísa nodded.

'Did you know about her?'

'Yes. I was the only one who did. I knew why Elín moved to Ísafjördur, but she wouldn't let me visit her there. No one else was to know. How old would she be now? Wait a minute . . . forty-six, I suppose. I've never met her. How did you track her down?'

'She was the woman who took the interview.'

Lovísa smiled at this.

'Typical Elín. Always a surprise twist at the end.'

'Who was her father?'

Lovísa looked at Helgi, her eyebrows raised in surprise.

'Isn't it obvious? She's Thor's child, of course. Thor was always the great love of Elín's life. Look, she may have written crime novels, but her own life was more of a tragedy, because all she wanted was to be with Thor. They were together before he met Rut. And they got back together for a while later on – he cheated on Rut and Elín got pregnant. But then Thor made it clear to her that it could never work. *Never.* That's an awfully strong word, Helgi. She never found anyone else; she was always single after that. Whereas I had a family, despite all my sins. You have to go on fighting, don't you? Live life to the full.'

Helgi suddenly saw Elín in a different light. He remembered the author photo on the back cover of her first book, the one he had read on the plane, and now he felt he perceived a sadness behind that ghost of a smile. Had she truly never got over her first love?

Had she given up her child to protect the man she loved . . .

He wished he could meet her and tell her to pull herself together, break out of her shell, make contact with her daughter, find someone to love – as he had found Aníta. Often it turned out that there was something to look forward to just around the next corner.

He tried again: 'Is Elín alive?'

This time Lovísa shook her head.

'No, she's dead.'

'Did you send the manuscript to Rut?'

'Yes. I found it at Elín's house. I wanted you to believe she was still alive. I even took away some of her post and newspapers so it would look as if she hadn't been missing as long as she had. A desperate attempt to delay the inevitable. You see, I knew – as you're clearly aware – that the interview was to be published on Elín's death, so it was hugely important to me that she should be presumed missing, not dead . . .'

'When did she die?'

'We went on a hike. I told you – and other people afterwards – that we'd climbed up Esja and come down again. Plain and simple. In reality, we went a bit further, up to Lake Hagavatn. It was supposed to be a two-day trip, with a night in the hut there.'

'Was it always your intention to . . .' Helgi paused for breath. In spite of everything, it wasn't easy to accuse this dignified woman of a second murder. 'Did you choose the place deliberately with that in mind – that Elín was to die there?'

His question seemed to shock Lovísa.

'What?' she exclaimed. 'No, you've misunderstood everything, Helgi.'

'Have I?'

'I didn't kill Elín – are you mad? She was my best friend.'

'And you knew, of course, that her death would in all likelihood lead to the publication of the interview, and the exposure of your secret.'

Lovísa shrugged.

'Yes, I suppose so, but that's irrelevant . . . We were so close – we were like sisters. No, what actually happened was that the hike was too much for her and she had a heart attack. We didn't have a phone signal there. I tried to save her, did everything I could, but . . . she just died in my arms. My dear friend.'

'Wait a minute . . .'

'I left her behind. I . . . Nothing more could be done for her.'

'Do you know where she is, then?'

'Of course I do,' Lovísa replied, as though it went without saying. 'It's pretty remote, but I tried to get her body into a sheltered place. I can lead the police to the spot.'

'Yes, please do that. We'll try and go first thing tomorrow, as soon as it's light.'

Helgi finished the last of his coffee, then rose to his feet.

'Lovísa, you know you're going to have to come with me now.'

She nodded.

'I suspected as much.'

'I'm sorry,' he blurted out, to his own surprise. Somehow he hadn't pictured the story ending like this.

Elín was dead.

That wasn't so unexpected, but he hadn't imagined he would have to escort Lovísa to the police station to be arrested.

It was clear now that Kristín would never have a chance to get to know her mother.

Yet he thought there was one small bright spot in the gloom – in all this rain – and that was that Elín's body would be found. Meaning that it would be possible to draw a line under the case and then her daughter would get her inheritance.

'Can I take a few essentials with me?' Lovísa asked, sounding like a frail old woman now.

'I'm afraid not. We need to get going.'

She smiled wearily and followed him out into the deluge.

He felt grateful that the day was drawing to a close.

1978

Christmas was coming, and Hulda's mind was almost entirely taken up with preparations for the imminent festivities.

It was Saturday and she had the day off, so she was walking along Laugavegur with Dimma. The little girl was four now and strutted along as though she owned the pavement, in between resting her weary legs in the pushchair. This was the life Hulda had wished for. She had realized that long ago and tried regularly to remind herself of the fact: a peaceful home life with her daughter and Jón.

Sometimes achieving happiness didn't have to be complicated, though of course she knew it was a privilege to enjoy the financial security that Jón's property business ensured them. They didn't have to watch every króna and were never broke when the end of the month came round, unlike so many of her colleagues in the police.

She smiled as she watched Dimma.

The weather wasn't actually that seasonal; it had started raining, but the excitement in the little girl's face conveyed more Christmas spirit than any snow. Hulda was so proud of Dimma. She was quite proud of herself too, as earlier that year she had finally managed to secure a job in CID. It had been a real uphill struggle and she had suffered a few setbacks on the way but, in the end, they hadn't been able to pass her over. She knew she was both perceptive and efficient, the equal of any of the men. It was lonely at times being the only woman in that environment, but she had long ago made up her mind not to let it affect her. She turned up to work every day with a smile on her face and wasn't going to let the hostility of her colleagues put her off her stride. She was determined to work her way up until one day she took charge of CID. It might be a lofty goal, but she was confident that she would succeed. All it required was ambition and tenacity.

At this moment, though, her goal was a more mundane one: to find a suitable Christmas present for Jón. It wouldn't be easy. He was always buying himself the latest gadgets, like a colour TV, for example. She would have liked to give him a book, though he only really read paperwork and contracts. But he had shown an interest in the latest thriller by Desmond Bagley, so Hulda had bought a copy for him. Jón had been a bit out of sorts in recent weeks, uncommunicative and curt with her, but she assumed the mood would pass.

In spite of looking forward to Christmas, she felt rather flat, as she often did at this time of year. Perhaps it was the December rain that had brought on her despondent mood, or perhaps it was that she felt the absence of her father more acutely as Christmas drew near. It was odd that she should feel this way, given that she had never actually met him. He was a shadowy figure in her life, yet paradoxically the idea of him seemed all-encompassing and warm. She often wondered how he spent his days and what it would have been like to grow up with him and celebrate Christmas with him. He was American and had been a member of the US garrison at the Keflavík Air Base, but she knew nothing else about him as her mother wouldn't reveal any more. No doubt he was still alive, somewhere on the other side of the Atlantic, preparing to spend the holiday with his family and friends.

She mustn't let these thoughts spoil her mood; the most important thing was to enjoy the holiday with her own little family. Dimma couldn't wait for Christmas, to put her shoes in the window every night for the thirteen Yule Lads to fill with presents in the run-up to the twenty-fourth, and all the other traditional festive trappings. With any luck the weather would improve too; what Hulda wouldn't give for some proper snow.

Sometimes, though, she suspected that her regrets about not knowing her father had more to do with an underlying fear of loneliness. She'd been assailed by an overpowering sense of dread during her visit to Elísabet, the widow of the man Einar Másson had killed: a dread of losing Dimma and Jón and being alone in the world again, as she had been during her first years in the infants' home – years she couldn't remember but which had left an indelible impression on her mind. Nothing could be worse than being left behind, alone and defenceless, with no one to turn to . . . That was why she always tried to make sure she had company when she went on her mountain hikes in the highlands. She couldn't bear the idea that no one had been there to take care of her during her first years and that the same could be true at the end of her life.

She made an effort to banish these thoughts as she and Dimma made their slow way down Laugavegur. The little girl was now asking for a ride in the pushchair. That was easily granted. Hulda carefully lowered Dimma into her seat and did up her harness.

She had a decent amount of leave over the holiday, though of course not a long period of consecutive days off since new members of CID couldn't expect this privilege. But hopefully it would allow her plenty of time to relax with her favourite people, read a book, watch something entertaining on TV and eat holiday food.

At that point the rain started coming down so heavily that Hulda was forced to take refuge in Adam, the gentlemen's outfitters. She hadn't planned on going in there, but it occurred to her she could maybe use the opportunity to buy Jón a scarf.

As she hurried through the doors, the world seemed to turn black for a moment, as though the clouds had swallowed her up as the heavens opened, and all she could think was: *we all die alone.*

2012

Tuesday, 6 November

Helgi had arranged to meet Rut at her publishing house.

She had invited him to her home in Laugardalur, but he didn't want to risk bumping into Thor. That whole story would have to wait for a more appropriate time.

He had no choice but to fill Rut in briefly on the outcome of the case. On the other hand, it wasn't essential for her to know that the journalist who had taken the fateful interview was Elín's daughter.

It was getting on for evening by now and all Helgi wanted was to go home, cook supper, then wait for Aníta to get back.

'Thanks for agreeing to see me,' he said to Rut. They were sitting in her office, surrounded by unpublished manuscripts. There was no one else at work this late in the afternoon.

'My pleasure,' she said, but he could detect a tremor

in her voice, as though she sensed that there had been a development and that the news was not good.

He came straight to the point.

'I'm sorry to have to tell you, Rut, but Elín is dead.'

He paused for Rut's response, but she only gasped and turned pale without saying a word.

'As far as we can establish, she died of natural causes – a heart attack in the mountains. She and Lovísa were on a hike together at the time.'

'What? I don't understand. Why didn't Lovísa say anything?'

Helgi chose his next words carefully.

'Because Lovísa didn't want the news to get out that Elín was dead.'

'For God's sake, why not?'

'Elín gave an interview some years ago in which she revealed an old secret. The condition she set the journalist was that the interview shouldn't be published in her – Elín's, that is – lifetime.'

'That's news to me. I had absolutely no idea about this.'

'I have to ask you a question, and may I remind you that you must answer truthfully.'

He saw Rut's hands twitching with agitation. She licked her dry lips, her distress obvious.

He resumed: 'What do you know about a bank robbery committed in 1965, for which a man called Einar Másson was convicted?'

'Well, I knew Einar, of course – he was a friend of Elín and Lovísa's, but . . . For goodness' sake, I know nothing about the robbery. It was a terrible shock to all of us when he was arrested. And it was awfully sad that he died so young.'

'What I'm going to tell you next is strictly confidential: Lovísa has confessed to having taken part in the robbery with Einar.'

'Lovísa? My Lovísa?'

Helgi nodded.

'No, that . . . that's impossible. It was two men.'

'Two masked robbers. One of whom was a woman.'

'No, no, not Lovísa. And why would you think Elín knew about it?'

'Elín knew what Lovísa and Einar were planning, and she wanted the truth to come out. In the end, that is.'

'Can I speak to Lovísa?' Rut asked.

'Not straight away. I assume she'll be charged with murder. She's guilty of causing a man's death. A cashier at the bank died in the robbery, as I expect you remember.'

Rut didn't seem to know what to say to this.

Helgi rose to his feet. 'I know this will be a big shock to you and your husband, Rut. I'm sure you'll get a chance to speak to Lovísa in due course. But I won't keep you any longer now.'

'Wasn't it Einar who shot the man?' Rut asked, her voice strained, as though everything was riding on the answer.

'Not according to Lovísa, I'm afraid. And I'm confident that she's going to have to face the consequences now.'

Rut's eyes were riveted on him, her face blank.

Helgi was at the door, saying goodbye, when she asked

in a voice that seemed to come from a long way off: 'Can I publish the book?'

He turned. 'What?'

'Elín's last book. I must be allowed to publish it.'

I suppose you'll have to ask her daughter, he was tempted to say, but he didn't want to get into that now. *Elín's daughter with Thor.*

Instead, he merely smiled at her, shrugged and said goodbye.

2012

Tuesday, 6 November

Once Helgi was sitting behind the wheel again, about to start the car and head home, he noticed that someone had tried to ring him. Looking the number up, he saw that it belonged to Elín's cousin, Orri, the university lecturer in the polo-neck jumper.

He sighed and decided to return the call while he was still parked. Come to think of it, he should probably also let Kristín know what had happened before the end of the day.

'Is that Helgi? From the police?'

'Yes, it is.'

'Ah, sorry to bother you. I just rang to ask if there was any news of my cousin.'

And her legacy, no doubt, Helgi thought cynically.

'It's a good thing you rang,' he said, 'as I was going to call you anyway. You see, there has been a rather unexpected development.'

'What? Is she dead?'

For a moment Helgi got the impression that Orri was hoping the answer to the question would be yes. That he would get his hands on all the wealth, though it would in fact never be his. Fate was playing a cruel game with the philosopher.

Helgi delayed answering as long as he could, before eventually replying: 'Yes, I'm afraid all the indications are that she died during a hike in the mountains. We're going to look for her body at first light tomorrow. I'm very sorry to have to tell you this.'

'Oh, that's terrible, absolutely terrible, but not entirely unexpected. Nothing else could have explained it. Poor, dear Ella.'

'It's also emerged that she had a daughter,' Helgi said, without stopping to think, but he couldn't control the urge to bring the philosopher back down to earth and make it brutally clear to him – if not in as many words – that he wouldn't be the sole heir to the bestselling author's fortune.

'I'm sorry? Who did?' Only now did Orri sound genuinely moved, even distressed, Helgi thought. But perhaps he was reading too much into the man's tone.

'Your cousin, Elín. We haven't quite got to the bottom of the matter yet, but everything will be clarified in the near future. It goes without saying that you must keep the news to yourself, but it seems you've got a cousin you weren't aware of.'

'That can't be possible, Helgi. There must be some mistake. Ella didn't have any children,' Orri said firmly.

'No, she didn't have any children, I'm absolutely sure of that.'

'Well, we'll see.'

'I refuse to believe it.'

'Anyway, I'm afraid I've got to run, Orri,' Helgi said, then added: 'By the way, I think you'd like her – Elín's daughter, I mean.' On the other hand, Helgi wasn't sure the feeling would be reciprocated.

He rang off, then immediately put through a call to Kristín. The car windows had misted up in the rain.

'Hello?' She sounded cheerful.

'Kristín? This is Helgi, from the police.'

'Oh, hello,' she said. 'How nice to hear from you again.'

'I went round to see Lovísa,' Helgi said, without elaborating.

'OK, right, I see . . .' After a pause, she asked: 'And did she kill Elín?'

'No, but Elín is dead.'

'OK.'

Helgi had been expecting a stronger reaction from her, although the news wouldn't necessarily come as a shock. After all, Kristín would never have a chance to see her mother again, never get an answer to all the personal questions she hadn't been permitted to ask during the interview. A disappointment she would no doubt deal with in private.

'We're going to retrieve her body tomorrow,' Helgi said, after a brief pause. 'If what Lovísa told me is true, Elín had a heart attack while they were in the mountains together.'

'Thank you for letting me know.'

'Let's talk properly tomorrow, Kristín, if that's OK. I realize there's a lot for you to take in. The inheritance, the interview – if you still want to publish it, given what's happened. Elín also left behind an unpublished manuscript, and I expect it'll be up to you to decide whether it should see the light of day.'

'Right, yes. And the funeral – maybe I can be involved with that in some capacity?'

'Yes, I'd have thought so. In due course, perhaps I can put you in touch with your mother's cousin, a university lecturer. He's her closest relative – was, I mean . . . You two should meet.'

'Yes.'

'Call me if you need anything, Kristín. Otherwise, shall we talk tomorrow?' Helgi was eager to head off home to the warmth and Aníta.

'Thanks for calling, Helgi.'

Then, belatedly, he remembered one more thing. 'Oh, yes. Listen, there was one other thing I meant to say.'

'Oh? What's that?'

'Lovísa told me who your father is. He's alive, still going strong. And he has two grown-up children, so you have a half-brother and -sister.'

2012

Tuesday, 6 November

This damned rain.

He couldn't concentrate. It was still pouring outside, the rhythmic pattering of the raindrops distracting him from *Brat Farrar*, the novel he was trying to read. The author, Josephine Tey, hadn't published many books, but, in his opinion, each novel had been better than its predecessor, and *Brat Farrar* was one of the only two books by her that he hadn't yet read. Tey's twists almost always took him by surprise and he was looking forward to seeing how she would pull the rug out from under his feet this time.

Yet he wasn't making any headway.

There was an appetizing smell spreading through the flat from the kitchen, where supper was waiting in the oven. Helgi had decided a special effort was called for to celebrate the occasion and had made a casserole, which was one of his signature dishes.

But it wasn't only the rain that distracted him now. He was preoccupied with the fallout from the day's revelations.

Lovísa would spend the night in a prison cell; the first of many, the way things were going.

And as soon as it got light tomorrow, they would be able to launch the search to retrieve Elín's body.

He had worries closer to home as well. His thoughts kept returning to his mother, who had rung him that morning to say she was feeling unusually poorly and was going to see the doctor that afternoon.

Filled with guilt at having cut short his visit to Akureyri, he had offered to fly north straight away, but she wouldn't hear of it. Anyway, he reminded himself, it would have been difficult for him to keep his promise, and his mother was an independent woman. She knew her own mind.

She had promised to ring him after her appointment with the doctor, but he still hadn't heard from her. Surely she must be out by now? It was nearly 6 p.m. and he was beginning to fret, but he held back from calling her as he wanted to give her a chance to let him know in her own time.

Aníta had gone out for a run. Far from being put off by the rain, she'd said she liked it. She hadn't brought up the subject of Bergthóra yet.

He sat there on the sofa with his book. He was in his favourite spot, embarking on a promising novel, savouring the peace and quiet in the knowledge that the mystery of the missing author had been solved – more or less – and he could look forward to the prospect of a relaxing evening with Aníta.

Everything he could have wished for, yet here he was, stuck on the same page.

His thoughts dwelled on Aníta. She always went out for a run at the same time, whatever the weather. She would be away for nearly half an hour, sometimes longer, and would return invigorated. They were out of sync in that respect. Where he himself often began the day by going for a run, she preferred to brave the elements, the cold, blustery Icelandic weather, after finishing work.

How he loved welcoming her back from those runs.

Thinking about Aníta and how much she meant to him brought it home to Helgi that he still hadn't got over the way Bergthóra had barged in on her at work. What an appalling lack of judgement. What embarrassing, disturbing behaviour. Was it possible that she had genuinely been stalking Aníta since then? The idea sent a shudder through him.

Unwilling to pursue this train of thought, he focused on his mother instead. Her illness, from which he hoped she'd recovered, despite today's slight setback, had made him more nostalgic than usual for his childhood. Scenes rose to his mind: the old, blue sofa in the sitting room at home in Akureyri and himself as a little boy, squeezed into the narrow space behind it that had been his lair.

His childhood had continued to exert a pull on him long after he had grown up, perhaps because it had taken him ages to work out exactly what he wanted to do as an adult. It was only now, with Aníta, that he felt as though he had come home.

With a little effort he could recall the smell of the sofa mingled with the aroma of the freshly made coffee that his mother habitually served to guests. His parents had never been that big on entertaining, but they'd had a few good friends who used to drop by regularly. And when they did, the conversation was often of books.

His father may have gone, but at least Helgi had recovered the bookshop. He wasn't remotely ready to lose his mother. Not for a long time yet.

Getting up from the sofa, he went through to the kitchen and put on some coffee.

He couldn't conjure up quite the same coffee aroma as he remembered from his youth; presumably his mother must have used a special brand, roasted and ground in Akureyri in those days. But the memory had given him a sudden longing for a cup, even though it was a bit late in the day for caffeine.

God, he hoped he would hear from his mother soon. He'd give her another hour, then he'd call her.

The coffee may not have been like his mother's, but it was good, strong and flavourful. And there was enough for a second cup. Aníta would appreciate that when she came in soaking wet from her run.

As if the coffee had released more positive feelings, Helgi became aware of a sense of pride in himself. The investigation had exceeded his expectations and he guessed that from now on he would be entrusted with bigger cases. Get the chance to grow and prosper in this job. Now that Elín's disappearance had been solved there were only a few minor cases on his desk, which he should be able to deal with during normal working hours in the coming weeks. He hadn't forgotten about Hulda either. Although he had never met her, the ghost of her presence still seemed to hang over the office.

Meeting Pétur had had a profound effect on him; seeing the grief reflected in his eyes, hearing the way he talked about Hulda. Clearly, she had been something of a pioneer among the women in CID, although she wasn't given any credit for the fact. There was one thing in particular that had continued to niggle at Helgi since his chat with Pétur, and that was the man's assertion that Hulda would never have deliberately disappeared. In other words, she wouldn't have killed herself. In spite of the age difference, it occurred to Helgi that she had been at the same stage in her life as him, taking her first steps in a promising new relationship.

As he stood there in the kitchen with a cup of steaming coffee in his hand, waiting for his girlfriend, he was aware of feeling happy. Hulda must have been feeling something like this. So why had she vanished? There were three possibilities: suicide, an accident or murder.

Suicide or an accident: neither seemed that likely. Hulda had been in the middle of an investigation, the last of her career. Judging by the notes in the case file, she had been busy with her inquiries and nowhere near ready to give up. What's more, she'd arranged to go on a date with Pétur. Why on earth would she have gone into the mountains alone, or indeed anywhere else where there was a risk of getting lost? It simply didn't make sense.

There was something more to this than met the eye. Helgi was sure of that. Perhaps he would allow himself a few days in between bigger assignments to make some inquiries of his own into Hulda's fate.

He glanced at the clock.

Aníta was due back any minute, after which the evening could properly begin. She always did the same circuit and usually kept up the same sort of pace.

He would drink a coffee with Aníta, then ring his mother for his peace of mind.

Now that he was feeling calmer, perhaps he would manage to read a few pages before Aníta got back. He would make a decent stab at getting into *Brat Farrar*. He was perfectly aware that his beloved books were yet another link to his childhood, another expression of nostalgia. The roots ran deep and he might as well face up to the fact.

These thoughts were dispelled by a knock at the door.

Aníta usually left it on the latch, saying she found it too annoying to run with a bunch of jingling house keys. She must have forgotten this time. But then no one's infallible.

He was crossing the flat to the door when he paused halfway, then turned back to pour a cup of coffee for his girlfriend. Aníta would be pleased by this thoughtful touch. A proper welcome. How different his life was now from the days when he was struggling to make it work with Bergthóra. There was such a lightness over everything.

Helgi hurried eagerly into the hall.

It wasn't Aníta.

2012

Tuesday, 6 November

There, smiling at him, stood Bergthóra.

Only a short time ago this would have been a perfectly normal sight. In another house, admittedly, and another life.

The unexpected visit threw him so badly that he couldn't stutter out a word.

He registered from the sudden burning sensation that he had spilt scalding coffee down himself. It had splashed his clothes, his trousers and shirt, and his bare arm.

Only a moment ago, the strong smell of coffee had conjured up such happy memories. But these evaporated in an instant, to be replaced by a chilling reality.

As the cup landed on the black floor tiles, Helgi heard the sound of it smashing, but he didn't glance down, just stared, stunned, at the woman in the doorway.

Somewhere in the flat he became aware of music playing. Oh yes, he had put a record on the stereo. But he had been so distracted by his thoughts that he had tuned it out. Now, though, to his suddenly acute hearing, it seemed amplified. Deafening even.

'Can I come in?' Bergthóra asked in an ominously flat, cold voice. It dawned on Helgi that he had probably never known Bergthóra. Not truly. He had lived with her and put up with her violence and drinking, but it seemed she had been hiding something else behind those problems.

'What?' Helgi said to win time, trying to grasp what was going on. Come to terms with the fact that it was Bergthóra, not Aníta, standing there in the doorway. He felt totally disorientated. Aníta was due any minute. The two women mustn't meet again; that was unthinkable.

'I asked if I could come in,' Bergthóra repeated, in a loud, clear voice, as though nothing could be more natural than for her to be there.

'No. We have nothing to discuss, Bergthóra,' he said, after a brief hesitation. 'Nothing at all. What the fuck are you doing here?'

'I just wanted to talk to you.' There was a look in her eyes that made his blood run cold. As if she wasn't really addressing her words to him. As if she was looking through him, talking into a void.

'You've got to leave,' he said firmly, taking a step backwards.

How the hell was he going to get rid of her?

He wasn't afraid of her; that wasn't the problem. She had used violence against him in the past, more than once, but he had usually managed to defend himself. He was stronger than her and she wouldn't be able to take him by surprise this time.

She must be drunk.

He was confident that he could contain the situation. She had already shown him her worst side in their relationship, so nothing she did now could take him by surprise.

He told himself he wasn't a victim any more. He didn't owe her anything – whereas she owed him rent.

But he had to get rid of her as quickly as possible.

The only question was whether he would be able to persuade her, whether she would come to her senses.

'Bergthóra, you have to go,' he repeated, when she continued standing there.

'No, I'm not going anywhere,' she answered coolly. 'I'm not budging an inch, Helgi.'

He stepped outside, pulling the door to behind him, wanting to deal with her in the open. Under no circumstances was he going to invite her into his new home. The air was raw out here and the rain that had been getting on his nerves all day long showed no signs of abating. He stood there in nothing but his shirtsleeves, braving the cold and trying to stay in the shelter of the shallow porch.

His thoughts flew to Aníta, who had chosen to go out in this. He peered into the darkness, trying to see if she was coming down the street. He didn't have much time.

'We have nothing to say to each other, Bergthóra. You've got to leave me alone. You should be grateful I didn't report you to the police.'

She smiled. 'Report me? What for? An accident? All

couples have rows.' She was soaked to the skin, but this didn't seem to bother her. She just stood there, immovable.

'Shall I call you a taxi, Bergthóra? You need to go home.'

'My home is with you, Helgi. And I don't need a fucking taxi. I drove here.'

'What?'

'I said: I drove here!'

'Just what is going on with you?' This was neither the time nor the place for a showdown, yet he was burning to bring up her visit to Aníta's workplace, the incident on the bus, and more. And not just to bring them up but bawl her out. Castigate her so savagely that she wouldn't dare repeat her behaviour.

'You – cheating on me like that.'

'*I did not cheat on you.* I finished with you, Bergthóra, after you tried to kill me.' He immediately regretted this reply. Getting into an argument with her was the worst thing he could do when she was in a mood like this. He had no hope of winning.

'If I'd meant to do that, I'd have succeeded,' she said menacingly.

'OK, now I'm calling the police.'

'You are the police, Helgi.'

This had to stop.

He could feel the fury boiling up inside him.

Bergthóra plainly had no intention of listening to him. Perhaps the only answer was to make good his threat and call the police. Thank God, neither of them had raised their voice, so with any luck the neighbours wouldn't have noticed anything yet. If only he could get rid of her.

Again, he scanned the street for Aníta.

'Expecting someone?' Bergthóra asked, in such an icy tone that her words sent a shiver through him.

He hesitated.

'I'm . . . I'm expecting a guest. You've got to go.'

'Well, well. A guest, is it? Who's coming round?'

Making a superhuman effort to control his anger, he pulled his phone from his pocket. 'I'm going to make that call, Bergthóra.'

'Were you expecting Aníta?' she asked, her voice dripping with spite.

'That's none of your fucking business, Bergthóra.' He selected the number of the police and prepared to call it.

'I know it was her,' Bergthóra said. Helgi, momentarily confused, looked up and caught her eye. God, she could be evil.

'Did you talk to her again, Bergthóra? Did you? You'd better leave her alone, or—'

'Or what?'

'Did you go and see her again? She told me you'd barged in on her at work, but . . .'

Bergthóra smiled. 'No, I won't be talking to her any more.'

Helgi felt a rush of relief.

'Right, well, let's keep it like that,' he said firmly, feeling for a moment as if he'd achieved the upper hand again. Though he knew this was rarely the case in their dealings.

'Yes, let's,' she said, disconcerting him.

Then she muttered something under her breath, the words drowned out by the noise of the rain.

'What? What did you say?'

For a second Helgi thought Bergthóra had given up and was saying goodbye. That he would be able to continue his evening as planned, almost as if this intrusion had never happened. There was no way Aníta would hear about Bergthóra's visit from him.

'I said . . .' She raised her voice: 'Aníta won't be coming now.'

'What do you mean?' His heart started pounding in his chest. 'Of course she's coming.'

'I drove into her,' Bergthóra said matter-of-factly. 'Just up the street from here.'

The words caught in Helgi's throat. He prayed he'd heard wrong. But he knew he hadn't.

'The visibility was so poor,' Bergthóra added, her voice suddenly so clear and calm that it occurred to him that she might not be drunk after all. She might even be stone-cold sober.

He was hit by a tidal wave of memories, an inexorable flood of images featuring Bergthóra, not Aníta, and all the terrible things he had let himself be subjected to without ever speaking up for himself. He had let her get away with her violence month after month, and failed to get a grip on the situation until it nearly ended in disaster. There had never been a real showdown. He had simply shut her out and tried to dismiss the terrible experiences from his mind, vacillating between guilt and sadness, then